PRAISE FOR

"With richly poetic details a
Nag captures his characters a
reflection. [*Hands Like Trees*]
stories by a writer to watch."

—ALIX OHLIN,
Giller-nominated novelist

"A sharp and incisive collection from a compelling new voice in Canadian fiction."

—ANNABEL LYON, winner of the
Rogers Writers' Trust Fiction Prize

"A totally engaging experience. We come away from these stories challenged and deepened."

—STEPHEN MORRISSEY, author of *The Green Archetypal Field of Poetry: on poetry, poets, and psyche*

"Satisfying is the only way to describe Nag's collection! These poignant stories, poetic in their detailed descriptions and flawed characters, highlight a life of challenges for those who have and those who have not and reflect a society where even class doesn't protect you from the realities of a disconnected or interrupted life. I walked away feeling as though I had entered another world, complicated, and wrapped up in so much societal expectation and tradition yet tainted by past experiences."

—STELLA HARVEY author of *Finding Callidora*,
The Brink of Freedom, and *Nicolai's Daughters*

"*Hands Like Trees* glows with life in every story. Here are characters that are complex, astute, painful, funny, enlightening and most of all enjoyable. Restless men and wilful women, who seek escape but also belonging, a contradiction and elusiveness that bursts with wit and empathy. These are nimble stories imbued with insight into the ties that bind, the ties that break, stories that shimmer with the soul of a poet. Cool and fierce, the power of Sabyasachi Nag's writing pulses with grace and maturity. A marvellous debut."

—JOHN VIGNA, author of *No Man's Land*

"Sabyasachi Nag's story cycle, *Hands Like Trees*, is Arundhati Roy as if written in the mode of Alice Munro. Nag applies the vivid and surprising imagery of the author of *The God of Small Things*, that panoramic epic, to the photo-album, snapshot intimacy of the linked short story as in Munro's *Lives of Girls and Women*. But Nag presents herein the lives of 'New Canadians,' either born in Canada or arrived within living memory. No matter their origins—in India—or their locations—in the Greater Toronto Area, their loves are complicated, while their lives mash up memory, dreams, nightmares, and fancies. Nag is a masterful writer, presenting the oddities of here and the eccentricities of there. The migrant seeks Oz, but ends up in a Twilight Zone of the slippage between promise and fate, possibility and doom. In such a situation, the real becomes surreal, and characters are only as sensible as they are quirky. This story collection recalls both James Baldwin and Bharati Mukherjee, but is unforgettable in 'Sach' Nag's own 'write.'"

—GEORGE ELLIOTT CLARKE, author of
Where Beauty Survived: An Africadian Memoir

"The book maps a strange physics of existence. Reading it in one stretch was like peeking into the chamber of a particle collider. The characters move damagedly in worlds of existential dread. They fear that their secrets will be discovered. They seem to speak in 'slightly different dialects about the same set of things'... There are no havens. A distaste for the physical underlies these worlds illustrated in the still life of 'the turkey and the meats, the peeled potato and broccoli rotting on the kitchen table.' Bodies decay with age, disease, alcohol, and abuse ... I admire the skills with which the narratives move back and forward and many times sideways through different temporalities and perspectives and the switch from diegesis to sudden interiority."

—AHMAD SAIDULLAH,
author of *Happiness and Other Disorders*

"The stories in *Hands Like Trees* evoke a vivid, often disquieting world. Moving deftly from character to character, Sabyasachi Nag draws us deep inside a tangle of kinship to reveal secrets both guarded and shared. A fresh and fearless collection."

—ALISSA YORK, author of *Far Cry*

HANDS **LIKE** TREES

HANDS LIKE TREES

A story cycle

Sabyasachi Nag

RONSDALE PRESS

HANDS LIKE TREES

RONSDALE PRESS
125A–1030 Denman Street, Vancouver, B.C. Canada V6G 2M6
www.ronsdalepress.com

Typesetting: Julie Cochrane, in Caslon 11 pt on 16
Cover Design: David Lester

Ronsdale Press wishes to thank the following for their support of its publishing program: the Canada Council for the Arts, the Government of Canada, the British Columbia Arts Council, and the Province of British Columbia through the British Columbia Book Publishing Tax Credit program.

Library and Archives Canada Cataloguing in Publication

Title: Hands like trees / Sabyasachi Nag.
Names: Nag, Sabyasachi, 1968- author.
Description: Short stories.
Identifiers: Canadiana (print) 20230156770 | Canadiana (ebook) 20230156797 | ISBN 9781553806868 (softcover) | ISBN 9781553806882 (PDF) | ISBN 9781553806875 (EPUB)
Classification: LCC PS8627.A483 H36 2023 | DDC C813/.6—dc23

At Ronsdale Press we are committed to protecting the environment. To this end we are working with Canopy and printers to phase out our use of paper produced from ancient forests. This book is one step towards that goal.

Printed in Canada

FOR ASIFA BANO

(2010–2018)

CONTENTS

1992

SOMEWHERE IN NORTHERN INDIA

~AURO

The Man and the Boy

I don't think any of this would have happened if Milli hadn't insisted we fly up to Rishikesh in the Himalayas and receive blessings from Mata G., her family's spiritual guru for two generations. She had another miscarriage last year, and we have been married for five years. And she wants a family. "I'm running out of time," she says. She's only thirty-three.

Here at the ashram, they teach you how to breathe, love, grieve. We're exhausted. We don't see anyone before checking out. Not even each other until we're on the train heading to Calcutta, where I'll have to resume the difficult task of persuading my father to wrap up his affairs and join us in our new home in Brampton, Ontario. We're both looking out the window at the porch lights shining outside low brick houses; level crossings; fields washed in rain—a quilt of dark, wet green—dark clover or avocado—interrupted by scarecrows, bridged by a network of narrow mud roads shining under the moon, heading to the vast darkness covered in haze. Milli was born in Calcutta but grew up in the Middle East. I'm visiting after many years. In a way we're both strangers in the country. At the station, you can smell the food—samosas, chaat, aloo tikki.

A man and a boy get on, bent over, hauling what looks like a heavy tin trunk, panting for breath after what seems like a mad sprint, up then down a winding overpass from nowhere to nowhere. The train had pulled in moments earlier. It would leave in a moment. They seem to be sweating, or perhaps it's the rain.

The boy is twelve or thirteen. From his smooth-as-pebble face, it's hard to tell. He's wearing a white Muslim cap like the older man. The man's eyes never rest on anything, move up, down, and sideways, inside deep sockets framed in dark circles; he seems to be searching for something.

It's after eleven. The night is spread out like a coat of black butter. We pass the outer fringes of Lucknow, the cultural mecca of medieval India. The train is running on time. The man and the boy struggle to pull the trunk through the narrow corridors of the train car. Two bunk berths face each other across the width of the train car, and a bunk berth on the side runs the length like a spine, splitting the coach into compartments, each compartment holding six sleepers—a universe with a courtyard in between. Within the compartment, there are no hard partitions or divides, just curtains. The lights are coming on and off.

The man and the boy stop across from our compartment. They face the bunk berth on the side. It seems they've booked both berths, but the berths are taken by two men facing away. The squatters are fast asleep. They don't notice the arrival of the man and the boy. Every other seat is taken. Everywhere there is someone already. They try to move our things under the berth so they can jam their trunk somewhere, forget about whatever is in it. There is no room. The trunk is too big.

The conductor is already heading their way. He wears dark pants and white sneakers. He has a dark jacket on. Nothing fancy, the kind people wear with shiny nickel buttons and shoulder loops to give an impression of authority. Seeing him, the man gets busy, rummaging through the deep pockets of his dark tunic for the tickets. The conductor taps at the knee of the squatter on the lower berth. The squatter doesn't move; he's dead-still. But the man and the boy wait. They've nowhere else to go. The conductor's hand rocks the squatter's body, bringing it back to life.

The lower half of the conductor's face, barring the space between the nose and the upper lip, is covered in a rich growth of white beard that he has dyed in places, the kind of orange you get on your hands after slicing fresh turmeric. He has shoulder-length hair, brushed from the flanks above his sideburns towards the centre of his head to hide a gaping bald patch. He looks over fifty. He's chewing betel. The squatter in the lower berth suddenly kicks at the conductor, who is jabbing a clipboard into his feet. The clipboard goes flying. The boy picks it up.

"This seat is reserved. Please find something else." The conductor's tone is polite, respectful. It seems he's used to being treated this way, or he knows something that makes him respect the squatter.

"This seat is taken," the squatter says. "*You* find something else."The squatter's strong voice has shaken Milli out of deep thought. She turns away from the window, looks at him. The squatter is facing away, towards the window on his side of the night. The window with Milli's reflection is dotted with splashes of rain. The rain flashes like cinder as the train passes random light posts.

The conductor is firm; the squatter won't let go. People crane their necks to check in on the strange spectacle of two grown men arguing over a seat. The man and the boy watch the conductor, who's doing most of the talking. Milli, wide awake now, watches the boy.

She had stayed up the previous night smoking hash from a hookah between moments of extreme clarity. I did, too. I know how it feels—the taste of metal on the mouthpiece, the rumble of the water jar before the jack-up from the dark pit. Even if it's just for ten minutes. I know she was making something of it, the whole week, breaking up the darkness into small, manageable pieces. I know she's right on the edge. I look at her hands. She has the hands of an artist—veins spread across the back, like roots, dirt lined up in her gnawed nails: dirt from all the digging and planting all week. *Trees—like babies*. Jujube mainly, that's what she planted into the dirt, into the void, because they live a hundred years and start fruiting at two. *One sure way to become a grandma really quick.*

Her eyes are closed. Her body sways to the wobble of

the train car. Her lips open and shut, purple from all the pot we smoked all week. Her shiny hair, parted on two sides like a railroad cutting straight into the sky, blurred, as it trails down the horizon. I can't see that far, but I know. Right now, she has started to speak a strange cocktail of Hindi, thick with Brampton North Park Canuck, her voice just as strong as the squatter across the aisle. She can't help it. "Can you men take it outside?"

What she means—*Let the boy sit, you assholes.* They don't get that, of course. Or maybe they do, and they don't care. Or maybe they care, but they like her talking to them that way.

The train has caught speed past a tiny lightless substation. I usually remember place names, but I'm looking at the boy—if Milli hadn't suffered a miscarriage, our first child would be his age. His brown eyes move gently, touching everything. He's curious. He's waiting for his seat. The squatters don't care what the conductor says. The conductor needs help. It's clear. It'll be an hour and a half before the train reaches a terminus big enough to have lights, big enough for the conductor to find someone to help him do his job. Or perhaps there's help on the train waiting to be called up.

The late monsoon has cooled the ground outside. You can tell from the smell. A chilly draft whistles in through cracks around the sealed glass. The wobble rocks the boy's hair. He has the round face of a sand pebble. I said that already. The pebble has been chiselled and sculpted by a wild torrent for a long time.

"We can use another seat, you know." The man is quick on compromise. "Any seat. Anywhere else. We're all passengers, aren't we, every one of us?" He looks at Milli, for affirmation, I think. Or perhaps he's embarrassed. "It's only a matter of a night."

I know what Milli is thinking. She thinks he's a loser. I think he's playing nice, trying to make a deal, get back to being invisible. Milli doesn't understand that. She's a straight shooter.

Just when it seems the man is ready to go away, she opens her mouth. "Hello. You booked this seat, right? And this boy here has been standing, waiting?"

The man with the cap looks at her, annoyed, as if she spoke out of turn. And that's when everyone hears it, too—they stir on their seats, crane their necks again. A crack starts someplace you can't see, and then a ripple of cracks as people move in their sleeper bunks just to get a closer look at Milli.

"Is this your seat?" she asks the boy. The boy nods. "That man stole it. Right? Steal it right back."

The boy says nothing.

"Take it."

No one says anything.

"Come on. Take it," the squatter in the lower bunk berth calmly says. *Sotto voce*. Like a doctor breaking bad news. He straightens himself against the window, looks across the aisle towards Milli. Her eyes are brown, almost like split cobnut with a blue-black husk in the shape of eyelashes.

Some kind of a turn-on for him, I guess. He leans back on the window, flings his cracked feet the entire length of the corridor right up to the edge of my seat, crosses his arms as if to say, *You don't even belong here, you shitheads.*

Then he turns towards the man, the boy, and the conductor, stopping to observe them carefully, making a show of the care with which he observes. I can tell he's looking at the unusual arrangement of the conductor's hair, connecting the turmeric-orange of his beard to the Muslim cap on the man and the boy. I know. I've made that connection. I know what he's doing.

"You guys related? You guys brothers?" he says, clapping the seat, making a big show of trying to stop himself from falling over in fake glee—laughing at his finder's luck as though it's a life-altering discovery.

"Let's go. We don't want trouble." The man is not looking at the squatter but at the conductor, this bearded train official, as if they were both tagged in some unspoken way, in singular distress. "Is there another place we can use? For the boy? I mean, just the boy. He can't be standing up the whole night."

The man now looks at Milli and keeps looking, as though, just by looking, he could evoke a response.

"Don't do that," Milli says to the man.

As the man shuffles, the squatter grabs the boy by his arm, draws him close to his face. The boy is short. "Show me your ticket," he says.

"The ticket is with him." The boy points at the man.

"Come on. Pull it out." The squatter reaches for the man, staring into his eyes, not the way he was staring at Milli. It's different.

"That's my business, mister." The conductor steps in, now with an acid voice. He's going to cut the squatter into pieces with his words.

"I don't like how you smell, man. Get away from me," the squatter says to the conductor. "You've been eating something terrible. I can tell just from the colour of that thing on your face, man. You want me to be sick? In your face? Just get the hell out. And . . . don't open that mouth again."

The conductor says nothing to the insult. He doesn't want to be provoked.

"Why don't you just let the boy have his seat?" Milli says.

"Veeru, you hear that?" The squatter in the lower berth slaps the seat again with his palm like he did a while back, like a child working a rattle. "Your wife?" he asks me with a wink.

I know what he's asking, but I suddenly feel the need to protect everything from him. I do a head bobble just to throw him off. I don't want to tell him anything. Maybe it's a mistake. It trips a fuse inside Milli's head. I can tell.

"Talk to me," she says to the squatter.

The night's raging outside, lights are coming on and off past abandoned outposts in the middle of nowhere. Other than the chemical buzz of the fluorescent, there is nothing else—not even the rattle of the train car. The sound of steel on steel has now settled deep inside the ear, like a worm.

"Your friend or wife?" the squatter asks me again. Then he says, not to me but to the man on the upper bunk berth, "You up or what?" Not waiting for an answer, he taps the upper berth with his foot, hard, exactly where the other squatter is resting his head. He must know what he's doing because the kick wakes up the squatter above.

That's when I realize what the conductor has been trying to do. He knows the squatters are together.

"Why don't you go call the cops?" Milli asks the conductor. "What are you waiting for?" She moves her face towards the squatter as if to point the threat at his head. As if she has found a gun and is going to blow his brains out.

"Why don't you go call the cops?" the squatter repeats after her, *sotto voce*, like before. "What are you waiting for?" He looks at Milli, then back at the conductor accusingly, as if the conductor has been delinquent at something he needed to have done long back—bringing these tourists up to speed with how things work here.

At first, I sense sarcasm—or scorn, perhaps. And then I look at the conductor, his unruffled manner, prepared for every spin and turn, almost rehearsed, and the thought strikes from nowhere—what if all of this is rigged? What if the conductor is the real faker? What if the boy's seat was sold long before the train even started and what we're witnessing is just a show?

The conductor gestures for Milli to stop. He doesn't

want to leave anyone in doubt that he's in control. Shaking his clipboard at the squatter, he says something I can't hear. He's a fast talker. I don't understand. Or perhaps he began saying something, and then the train car wobbled, and he bit his tongue.

The man up top has now moved. He's looking at Milli from his perch. I know his name is Veeru. When I was younger, that name had the same effect as Butch Cassidy from the Hollywood film. He stretches his legs under a white sheet spotty with brown stains. The stained sheet is crumpled against the blue rexine on the cushioned upper berth. He watches Milli from his perch and moves his hand rapidly under the sheet, never losing eye contact. She looks away. He laughs.

"You drink, brother?" Veeru asks the conductor. "I got whisky."

They laugh, both men on the bunk berth across the aisle, a guttural laugh.

"I'll give it to you neat, bro. No water, no soda, no nothing. Just go back to where you came from. Take your things. Hello. Take your things and take your brothers. I don't want you here. You understand? I'll bring it to you in a cup. No shit. I promise. You said you want *no trouble.* Right? *No trouble?* Just go back."

There is a strange authority in his voice. It makes the man with the white cap look towards the exit. Perhaps he remembers something—evening news packed with images of a mosque being dismantled, bloody faces of men and boys—many wearing the Muslim cap, this same white, like the boy, framed to the black of the hairy head and full of holes—fighting, flailing about, falling. Perhaps the man knows something. He turns and walks towards the door, and the conductor follows. I look at the boy. I want to say to him, *it happens*. I mean, it has happened before with other people, elsewhere. No big deal. But Milli has gotten a hold of him, the boy who started to follow the men. The boy is now torn. He seems to like Milli or likes being held that way. He looks up into her brown cobnut eyes. Perhaps he can see something no one else can.

"You stay here!" She straightens herself on the seat, making room. "Why are you following the men? You're not a man yet."

The boy looks at her, stunned, as though he can sense something in her voice that he wants to keep even though she isn't making sense to him.

"Here." She draws him close and hands her phone to me. "Call the emergency number," she asks me, foraging in her leather pouch as if she means what she said, as if she really has a number on her. Then she grabs her thick-rimmed black eyeglasses, shaped like a trapezoid, clearly too big for her lean face.

"You need a number to call, bro?" Veeru looks at me from his perch, his eyebrows cocked, eyes shifting towards Milli. He seems to be in charge. I can tell he knows something. He's now crouched against the ceiling of the train. He has uncrossed his arms. His cracked feet hang down the bunk berth. He's leaning forward, ready to pounce, I think, if I make one wrong move. He's strong. I notice the bulge of his frame bursting from his slim-fitted brown half-shirt.

Something about the way he says those words, the cold, ratchet pitch of a jackhammer breaking concrete, makes the conductor stop and turn around. "Do you really want the cops?" he says, drawing closer to this man on the top berth, looking him in the eye. There is something they both know, but the conductor no longer cares.

"You hear him, Jai?" Veeru says, punctuating his words with a sound one makes blowing dirt into a snot rag. The squatters have found a game. They want the conductor gassed up like a tube man before they bring him down.

"Come here," Veeru says, staring down the conductor from his perch, gesturing at his thigh as if inviting him to an act they both know well. The conductor says nothing to the insult. Meanwhile, Jai has flanked his legs around the conductor, jamming them to the steel ladder on the bunk berth across the aisle. Girdled between Jai's legs, the conductor is frozen, helpless, without a voice. He looks at Milli, looks at the boy, looks a few feet away at the man near the exit.

"Here, come on, do it," Veeru says, repeating the gesture around his thighs. The conductor ignores him, tries forcing himself past Jai's flanked legs. Those are strong legs.

"You come this way, brother," the man says to the conductor. He has come up the aisle to fetch him, but he's looking at the squatter on the lower seat, the man called

Jai. The man looks at Jai and shakes his legs wedged around the conductor, shakes and stops, shakes again and stops, as though begging him to let go. *Let go. Please. I beg you. We'll be gone. Forever. Into the night.* Jai lets go. The conductor and this man with the cap walk towards the exit, one trailing the other, without a word. But the boy doesn't move. He stays.

Milli is looking out the window. The wind is slapping in the rain hard. You think you can hear the rain even though the sound of steel has absorbed what it can. "What's inside the box?" Jai asks the boy.

"You don't have to answer that." Milli turns to face the boy. "Where's your mother?" she asks as if that, instead, was the right question.

"She's gone," the boy says.

"That man? He's your father?"

The boy nods, looks at Milli, hesitates as if he's unsure.

"Gone where?" she asks again.

The boy doesn't reply.

"And where are you headed?"

"To my new home."

"How long ago was she gone, your mother?" Milli asks.

"I don't know. I was sleeping."

"Gone, just like that?

"My grandma said someone shot her."

"Really? Shot her? Who?" Milli says.

"Then the man came."

"You mean that man? So he's not your father?"

"Grandma says I should call him Father."

"You never saw him before? And your granny let you go?"

"She said there was nothing for me to stay back for. She said I have to make my journey, claim what's mine."

"She didn't want to come with you?"

"She's old. She can't go anywhere. Besides, she said it was not her place. I have to do it alone."

"What are you going to claim?"

"My grandma said my great-grandfather used to be emperor."

"Of what?"

"You see that?" He points out the window. "All of that."

"All of it?"

"The entire thing. And then he went east. To Calcutta."

"And that's what your granny says you should do? Claim all of that? And what was the emperor's name? This emperor has a name?"

"Emperor Wajid Ali Shah."

"Yeah? From history," I ask.

"Yes."

"The emperor who danced to his own score?" I look at the boy, then towards Milli. "I read stories about him when I was younger—he had three hundred and seventy-five wives." I like where the boy has led us, but I don't believe him.

"Open it," Jai interrupts, kicking at the tin trunk.

"Ignore him," Milli says. "And you've seen him? You have a photo?"

"I don't have the key." The boy looks at Milli.

"Yeah?" Milli blurts out loud, amazed. "Really?"

"Everyone at home dances. Even my grandma. We're the family of Wajid Ali Shah. It's in my blood."

Everyone laughs. At the boy. At what he just said. At the anklets that he has now taken hold of, that he's now holding out for everyone to see. Milli looks at them in disbelief. I can tell from her eyes. I know what's going through her mind. She likes the boy. She wants to keep the boy. She laughs and holds on to the boy.

"Do you want to come with me?" she says.

"Where?"

"To my home."

"Where is that?" the boy asks.

"It's on the other side of the world," Milli says.

He shakes his head sideways. "My world is here."

And she laughs. The hollow laugh of a penny in a tin can. I know that laugh. Strangely, everyone is laughing at the boy as he puts the black leather strap on his left foot, like someone who has done it countless times before. He does it without bothering to look—sliding the tiny prongs into the precise punch holes, easing the tips of the narrow belts into tiny loops just by touching them. He's about to repeat the act on his right foot. His face is washed in glory.

Just then, the man with the white cap shows up from nowhere. He sees the broken lock, the trunk forced open, the boy holding up a dancing anklet, ready to put it on. He pauses. I see his body shaking. I don't know if it's rage or shame or fear, but he's shaking like someone took his clothes and he's cold. He looks at the boy's foot, shiny with the metal bells on the strap he had put on before. The man reaches for him. The boy moves the other black strap between his tiny fingers, his face turned up towards the man, still smiling, hopeful, flushed with glory. The man takes the strap in his hand, as though it's rightfully his. Then he strikes the boy's face with it, so hard the boy falls over. In a stunning second, the man looks around, meeting everyone's eyes. The boy gets up and looks away, his pebble face darkened with the marks from the blow.

Before anyone realizes what happened, Veeru jumps down from the upper berth into the aisle, letting the full weight of his body bear on the shoulder of the man with the cap, instantly bringing him down to the floor.

And Jai, as if waiting for a cue, leaps out of his seat, lunges at the man sprawled on the floor. Then he starts dragging the man's body by the collar, towards the exit of the train. Veeru lifts the man by his feet, Jai drags him. Then they take turns to kick at the man's hands, which are trying to grab anything that comes his way—the tin trunk, the steel ladders, the steel of the bunk partitions, pleats of the curtains farther down the aisle. No one says a word.

By now, Milli has taken the boy in her arms, crudely, as though she has found what she has been missing all this time, as though it were for her to give the boy what he doesn't know belongs to him. And she doesn't know either, how to say it or even what to say. The boy is still. He's looking out the window, looking at the night outside as if it were his own. As if he has been out there before.

Jai and Veeru are still working on the man. They've

dragged him close to the exit. It seems they're going to throw him out of the train, without another word, as smoothly as if they've practiced it. They've been waiting. Everyone has been waiting—wanting it to be over fast so they can put it in the past and go back to sleep.

Just then the conductor hurries in. He holds on to Veeru's waist, trying to stop him. The conductor is strong. He wiggles his body into the steel of the bunks and tries to stall the squatters with everything he has. But the two men are unstoppable.

I look away. I look back at Milli. For a moment, I see her clenched jaw. For a moment, it seems she wants those squatters to do to the man what he did to the boy. The marks on the boy's face have settled.

On the far end of the train car, Jai is wrestling the door, trying to balance the weight of his body as he stands on the man's face, his cracked feet digging and twisting as he works the jammed bolts. And when the door flings open, a gust of wet air rushes in, and Jai, as if he were expecting something else, is thrown off; in the power of the wind, he meets his match.

The conductor stands watching Jai as he hurtles forward, face-first, out the train's open door like a straw man, halfway down the footboard, head popping out. Just a tap and he'd be on the roadbed—the rain-washed smoothness of the parallel tracks shining, vibrating.

Even in his fall, Jai has managed to wedge his legs onto the man's head, his crotch jammed against the man's neck, arms flailing for grip on the steel handle outside. He's so close to the girders, cinders from the train wheels fly out at his face.

The mad wind pulls them both down towards the cinders, the man's head wedged between Jai's legs. They're both slowly sliding. I stand behind the conductor, helpless, staring. Maybe that's how justice happens. I don't say it. But Jai's friend, this other man called Veeru, has now joined forces with the conductor, trying to stop the man with the cap from sliding down any further—the same man he was about to throw out of the train. By doing that, he thinks he can stop Jai from being blown into the wind. He holds on to the man's waist, winding up in knots against the walls of the train car, against the steel of ladders, against angles and poles, resisting the drag of gravity, the wind, resisting the spell of the parallel track hurrying past.

He and the conductor pin the man to the floor before pulling him back inside, the man with the cap, and with him, Jai, wrapped around his crotch like a chain lock. Then the two squatters, without another word, head back to their places. The man with the cap lies face-up on the floor. His jacket ripped, shoes off, tunic soaked in grime, blood oozing from his nose.

"The man's bleeding," someone says.

"I have first aid in my carry bag," the conductor says.

"You stay here with me," Milli says, refusing to let go of the boy's hand wrapped around hers. I notice the open trunk with the emperor's things getting in everyone's way. I pull it back inside.

1985

CALCUTTA

VISMA

Pumpkin Flowers

February in Calcutta is already spring. I'm still in bed. I know it's time. I don't have to look at the clock. Outside, it's dark; the air is heavy with dew. A strange glow from the streetlight hangs like sprayed paint over homeless men asleep on the unwashed pavement under the verandah running the length of the house. They don't have to worry about time. They sleep when they can, wake up when they have to. Not me. I worry. At sixty-five you worry. Especially now that Rita is gone. Toshie is gone. Auro is gone. They're all gone.

I should be out by now. Out there on the street doing what I do at this time—walking—with the steel-tipped chestnut stick Toshie got me from some quaint town in Canada where they still roll around in horse carts. There is a method to how I walk—there needs to be a method—briskly, past the block facing my house. I slow down at the corner facing the drugstore with the yellow gate and the butcher's, where stray dogs laze around all day. Then the post office, the laundry, the Zari store that's always locked, the library, and the *Barbar Shop* pointing towards Circus Park. On any other day, I'd make the three-kilometre stretch inside thirty minutes. Always the first to show up for Tai Chi with Ju Li. But today is not any other day.

Last night, I couldn't sleep thinking about Ju Li. All the crows outside have started cawing at the same time, interrupting the chatter of the car washers. I know the car washers. Something about them makes me nervous—that laughter—after one kicks a dog in the rib, the other laughs, then they both laugh. I try to get a closer look at the dog. I can hear my own heart. Pounding. Racing. Dhak-dhak. Dhak-dhak. I don't know. I'm of two minds—get out there or stay put.

It'd have been easier to decide if it wasn't for the pumpkin flowers. Dozens of them in the vines up on the terrace. I've promised to give them all to Ju Li. When it's time. Today is the time. I must get them off the vines today. I must get them now, under the cover of the dark, while they're still open. Soon the petals will close for the day—close and cling together as if they've been drained of the will to live. Then they'll dry. And then they'll be no good for anyone. Not for Ju Li, who wants them open, exactly like the one I gave her the first time, on a whim, just to see if she'd accept a flower from a stranger in the park with everyone watching. It wasn't a rose. It wasn't a lilac. Not an orchid. It was very early in the morning. She accepted the pumpkin flower, no questions asked. Now I'll give her the same flowers again—all the pumpkin flowers on the vines. I'll surprise her, and then I'll ask her out. I can ask her out without flowers. I know that. But I've never asked for anything without having something to give back. Why would I change that for Ju Li?

I get out of bed and rush to the bathroom. Lately, this damned bladder, it can hold nothing. Five feet ten, muscles and bones, yet nothing to hold. My face holds plenty: scars from wars—quarrels that will never make it to history books—and a grey walrus moustache. In the mirror, I look like a stranger in my own house, out on the streets, a stranger in my own town. The moustache is new. I started growing it after moving back here, to this house I was born in, back from the eleven years of commission in the military; the uniform still hangs in its original shape inside a shadow box next to the stacks of graded answer sheets collected over twenty-nine years of travelling all over the state, teaching high-school history. What a life! Dog's life. But dogs watch. They know a thing or two about time. And when you're rolling along like a sassy stray—and you've no doubt about the what and the why of all the rolling—you keep the taste of your history, even when you're brushing your teeth.

My moustache used to be jet black until a year back. Now that I've stopped dyeing it, it's as grey as the sky today, revealed in bursts through the flutter of the lace curtain on the open window. The moustache—when it was dark—worked like a coil spring. Not anymore. Now I have to use a stick when I am out there walking. That's how it is.

Since they left. But I don't want to be thinking about that today. Not today when I'm about to ask Ju Li out for tea, and my heart's failing me. Maybe if I dye the moustache it'll all change; the clock will get set back to the start again.

At sixty-five, the doctor said, it's not normal for the heart to be doing what it's doing today—firing up without warning and then shutting down, and then a stutter, and it's back again like an old chronograph running on empty. Not at all normal. Because I'm not running on empty. But why then am I wheezing and choking and swinging my hairy arms, gasping for air? Nothing I can do about it except to watch the sweat break along the deep lines on my neck, feel it crawling down the length of my spine, or hear the conch of my ear crackle with heat—tick-tock, tick-tock. I touch my earlobes. A shiver runs through my skull—a fierce shiver—as if something is hiding in there that will finally crack it open today. Then the shiver gets to my face, my entire body. I can feel the weight of my eyes, they're being pulled down by some invisible pendulum.

That's it, I say to myself. Talking helps. Suddenly the shivering stops. Everything returns to normal. Just like that. *That's it*, I say again, just to make sure it stays that way. But I can't forget about it yet—the chronograph-like stop and start—that's not what I thought my heart would become when I was young. I don't want the stop-start chronograph today. Just the heart. All the heart I can have, to clip the flowers when they're still young and open, and hand them all to Ju Li and ask her out. I'll do whatever it takes, keep talking as long as I can.

Almost twenty years ago when the stop-start first showed, the doctor said it's not normal for a forty-five-year-old to have a heart that stutters. That's what doctors say—cut the booze, cut the smoke, take your time, walk. So I've been walking. But nothing seems to have changed how the heart works. *Keep an aspirin with you at all times.* And now I'm dragging my hundred-and-eighty-pound body to the dresser, pulling out an old aluminum case. Soon I'll chew down a couple of aspirins and talk myself back to my feet. That will do it. It has always worked.

Now I can feel my knees. Sore but intact. I want to get outside now while everyone is still asleep. The strays out on the street are still barking. They've been barking all night as if something terrible has been happening to them, and they need someone to witness it. My ears are hot, the barking is loud and constant, now getting louder. There seems to be a connection; the walls keep closing in as the barking gets louder until there is no room left, even to breathe. I need to get out.

But how? The stick is at the cobbler's getting a leather cap nailed to its steel tip. I need the leather cap. Earlier it didn't matter, but now that they've left, I can't stand the loud metallic sound of the steel tip every time it strikes the concrete floor. I don't want anyone to know I'm walking away. I want them to know I'm here.

I can have the stick back only later. Tomorrow? *Maybe.* What about now? I need something to keep those dogs away—rabid as strays can be. They scare me—their strayness more than their dog-ness. I've been a dog before.

Many times, to many people. But never a stray. Not until now. When everyone is gone. I need something to support my knees; they're not what they used to be. The umbrella will do. Today it has to be the umbrella or nothing.

The dogs shut up after a while. But the heart keeps slamming into the chest and stopping, as if it has been forced into a cavity in the chest and gotten stuck—like a magnet—before releasing, settling back in place, restarting. The walk to the park might make it worse. Or better. No one knows how the heart works.

"Tomorrow," I say out loud as if someone is out there waiting on the balcony just to record those words so they might be played back to me in time. It's the bladder again. I get out of bed and rush to the bathroom. When I return, the chill blowing in through the bedroom window hits me on the bare chest. Sharp like a razor. I switch off the fan and slide back under the wool blanket Toshie brought me from a store in Canada where they let you walk around and try things on before you buy anything. The blanket is mighty warm. It's two years old and hasn't changed one bit. Two years since Toshie came to visit. It was summer, just a few weeks after Rita fell in the bathroom and suffered a stroke.

"Who is there to care for her here?" Toshie took her away. "She'll get better; it's a matter of time." I can't forgive her for that.

What about me? I didn't say it. The very thought of snow makes me sick. Or I'd be there running my own convenience store like my brother. I've had my share of snow, seen it, lived it. In trenches—alone and with other men—waiting for gunfire, for blood, for someone to fall dead so we could come out of our hole and claim the body while it was still warm. I don't need snow. Dying's better when you know you're dying warm, in a friendly, lighted place. I don't want to die a stranger. And I don't want to die in the dark. And I don't want to die alone. But I'm not dying. I'm not going to die. Not just yet. I know my body. I know something in the body will tell me when it's time. It isn't that time yet.

I take a drink of water. Read myself to sleep. When I wake, I'm back worrying about those pumpkin flowers. I get out of bed, walk the three flights of high cement stairs up to the terrace garden, clip the pumpkin flowers off the vines—all of them—and lay them down on the table. Dead still. They look like a series of still-life paintings. I want to place them inside a plastic container, stow them away in the freezer. The cold will do it—keep them open forever. Stop time on its tracks. Freeze them in forever youth.

But what good is a frozen pumpkin flower? Would the scents stay? Won't the edges become brittle? Won't the petals freckle up in all that cold? I can always get a new bunch, can't I? I know where to find them. But the pumpkin flowers in the bazaar aren't the same as the ones I raised with my own hands, on my own terrace, with seeds imported from a nursery in Canada where they have trees in twenty-gallon pots laden with fruit. A current runs up my spine just looking at the flowers laid on the table, now moving in the breeze from the window—as if still breathing, still but not yet dead—any moment they could break form and start talking. So bright and so huge, just their grandeur makes them perfect for Ju Li. It's the seed. It's got to be the seed. I remember how I had to pester Auro just to have those seeds sent over—please, please, please—the magic seeds from a smiling, petite farmer in Hamilton, Ontario, Canada who showed off those huge pumpkins on TV.

"What seeds? What would you do with pumpkins that big in a terrace garden?" Auro knows nothing.

I remember the scarp with the couriers when the package of seeds was returned undelivered. I was out. Or it had arrived before time. No one could locate it for days. "Only God can tell where it has vanished to." I remember Auro never called back to find out if those seeds actually reached me. Perhaps he knew. Perhaps he tracked the package. And he never called to find out if the seeds were any good. Perhaps everything is good up there in the country of frozen time. But I'm here. I'm all right here.

And I need to be outside. Out of the bed, on my feet. I feel better already. There is no point staying buried in a wool blanket when I know I won't be able to get any sleep digging up memories I can do nothing about. The flowers would surely turn bad. The freezer makes a weird noise. It's not cooling as well as it did when it was new. I don't think it can freeze time, keep the flowers open. Now that they're clipped, I have to give them away today. I have no choice.

"Do it," I say out loud before going about a series of breathing rituals I have practiced since my time in the military. It has served me well, this effortless act of breathing—in-out, in-out, in-out. Woosh-huh. Woosh-huh. It could have helped Rita. If she had listened. The doctors said it was a stroke. They said the stroke happened before she fell in the bathroom. It was the fall that destroyed her left eye. It could have ended up a lot worse if I hadn't returned on time—"and a lot better had someone been around when it happened." Doctors! They tell you what you want to hear. I don't believe a word. So what if I wasn't home when it happened? I wouldn't have been with her in the bathroom.

"There is no point arguing about what led to what." Toshie can be cold when angry. Snotty. "I have to take her with me, or you'll fight to death." She was right. We had been fighting. "Just a few weeks, and everything will be okay." There she was wrong. Several months later, she said what I knew from the start, "Mother doesn't want to return."

"Why can't I talk to her?"

"You can't be there on your own when everyone else is here."

"Where did I go wrong?"

"Why do you always want me to take sides?"

Auro likes to be neutral. Aloof. He understands. "Things happen for a reason. You've taught history; you should know it."

In the thirty years of our marriage, Rita didn't leave me

for a day. How can anyone in their right mind think anything would ever be normal after she left? When I became sure she wouldn't return, I knew I had to find a method to deal with it. During the day, I kept all doors and windows shut. No more questions. *Why did it happen? How could I let it happen? What am I going to do next?* More than the questions, back then, I didn't know how to deal with those that were asking the questions—the entire clan—it seemed all the Sens from Shulut had crawled out of the woodwork to study my situation. Sometimes it seemed they were always there, hiding, waiting for their chance to pounce on me with a pointed question. Payback for a history teacher who never learned from history. "It has happened to others—those who left never returned—so how could you not know?" Not all of them even knew me that well. I swatted them out and then shut the doors. By night, things numbed down. Soaked in whisky, even a scratch feels like a wound, and as you drink more, the wound grows, hollows out, then suddenly it feels as if an organ has been removed. I don't want to talk about it.

Something else happened. For a brief period, my sense of time was gone. The desire to live, gone. If the past is not heading anywhere meaningful, then what's the point? I realized no one needed me, and I needed nothing. I started plotting ways to end all this in a methodical way. I rarely stepped out of the home other than to walk. Barely ate. But starvation only makes you weak, doesn't kill you. The breathing got worse. All of last year. And then in August, when Auro came home to have his Canadian residency visa stamped, I could see my son had grown up all of a sudden. There he was, wrapping up his affairs, collecting his stuff. His college was done. Now what?

"What do you expect?" The land of the magic pumpkin had opened up for him with an offer he couldn't refuse. *Of course, you can refuse. Of course, I need you here.* But how does one say such things to the son who says his history will be made elsewhere? He's an idiot. History makes you, or you make history?

"Come with us." Back then Auro didn't even know where I'd live if I had agreed to follow him. He, himself, was living in a rented basement. "I'm twenty-eight. What do you want, a palace?"

"Everyone should be hopeful," I said.

"Why can't you be like everyone else?" Auro was trying to be patient, reasonable.

"What is everyone else doing?" I was curious.

"Ask your own brother. You can do what Uncle Fatik is doing."

"I heard he stands all day selling cigarettes and ice?"

"There are other things you can do. You'll be closer to us. Won't that count for something? And we won't have to be worried about you all the time."

Why couldn't I do it?

"You can't expect everyone to change themselves so they can fit into your time of life."

Of course not. Who can argue against that? "You've your time. I've mine."

"What do you want from us? Pity?"

Auro knows nothing. But the words stung. I didn't take his calls again. I decided to sell the house. For a day, I thought I'd move back to the country—back to Shulut, where my father and my father's grandfather were born. Back to the place where all the history began. But Shulut? I thought again. *Who knows me there?* No one knows me here. And I know nothing of this other place where they claim they can freeze time.

Sell everything and set off on the road—that's what I decided. *Be a dog. Just like the strays. Sleep where you can. Bark some.* And then someone let the word out and realtors started calling all hours of the day. "Uncle. You're sitting on a goldmine. But do you know of anyone who has eaten gold?"

They knew exactly what I needed to do. They had no hesitation in telling me what they knew. But to be told what to do, and then to do what you're told, what kind of a coward would fall for that? I remember the last of the realtors.

"Visma Uncle, if you've a problem in your heart, it's a bad idea to live alone. Anything can happen at anytime. You'll be dead sick; no one will know." He was young and shameless. He had a funny way of letting each word drip out his pouted lips like lumps of sugar laced in cigarette smoke. *When all else fails, cloud it up with smoke and take it down with sweetness*—that's what they think when they're young.

"Uncle, you may not know this, but Auro and I went to school together. So what if your son isn't here? What am I here for? I'll buy this house off you and set you free. If you don't trust me, ask your son. Ask your daughter. Aunt Rita was like a second mother to me."

That's it. After that, everything converged as in Shiva's Ananda Tandava—the cologne on the young realtor's extra-fine voile shirt, the shine of fake concern on his liquor-puffy face, the sound of my own heart slamming against my chest like a tape recorder going backward—whoosh. I grabbed him by the sleeve and led him out the front door. Then I called Rahim Ali, a retired sepoy who was now a building contractor.

Then I found a method for counterattack: How to tell them I won't be gone without a fight—do exactly the opposite of what they tell you.

If they say "Be sensible, Pa. Do what everyone else is doing," just say, "I know what I want."

If they say, "What good could come from dying alone in this shithole," say, "I know what I want."

If they say, "History is a disease that troubles only the vain and the stupid," say, "I know what I want." Then they go away. For a long time. And so if my heart fails, and if I die here alone, it's all my fault. But I know I won't die today. Not today when I have the pumpkin flowers all cut up for Ju Li.

Between the breathing rituals—in out, in out—I look around. The whitewashed cement walls of the bedroom are now faintly flushed with the blue light from the open window. Every inch of all the three walls facing me—every flat surface that can hold any weight—has been fitted with a photo or a plaque or a trophy or a souvenir. "What's the point of this?" Keep the history close so you know why you're still here.

I inhale hard and deep. Between my breathing rituals, I remember Rahim Ali, my do-it-all right-hand man and his wife—I can't remember her name. But I remember how they gutted the house—it felt like reclaiming a lost city. They made it worthwhile for all the history to return, straightening out the plumbing and the wiring and the floors and ceilings and stairways. I remember the hours we spent choosing the paints before settling on the four shades of grey and ivory white for the walls and doors and hallways—the perfect backdrop—so that the walls could expand like the universe and everything nailed to it have a true chance of revealing itself in time. I remember how everything looked, felt, and smelled different after that. Even after Rahim Ali and his wife were gone. Long after I had pulled out whatever knick-knackery I could find inside trunks and boxes, drawers, cabinets, and closets—spoons and mugs, seals and flags, trinkets, quilts, and photo frames—from way past and near past—pulled them out from their tin graves and mounted them to the walls, one at a time. Almost three thousand feet of wall space, spanning three floors in the entire house, all turned into a canvas. All of it alive and whispering and beating with time, tick-tock, tick-tock. I didn't know I could do that.

But it's there, right in front of my eyes; no one can deny

it. All of this history now hung up like a grand fresco. There was no way I could have buried all this in a time capsule and travelled to the land of the giant pumpkin. So that's the answer. It took a rude realtor and a clever handyman to unpack it. *Why are you still here? Why can't you just pack up and leave?* I can't because there is no decent way to pack up history and leave. Because to leave history and pack up is not what my time here is all about. Time has a shape, direction. No one can freeze time in a pumpkin flower.

Frankly, I've no idea if she wants them. What would she do with them? About those pumpkin flowers, the only thing I can think of is to coat them in chickpea batter, make fritters out of them and crunch them down with tea. I'm not even sure if Ju Li knows how to make pumpkin flower frits the way my mother did, but Rita could never do—always searing them on the edges, bitter and useless. Perhaps Ju Li knows something about pumpkin flower fritters that no one else does. A recipe handed down in a secret scroll. But then, I don't know Ju Li at all.

At the park, they talk about Ju Li. I know what they talk about when they talk about Ju Li. They try to make her look like some kind of poison hemlock—get too close and you're dead. I don't trust that kind of talk. I know what I know. Ju Li lives alone. That's enough. They say her dead husband left her in debt. They say she has to rent out every room in her house to strangers and drifters to make ends meet. That's what they say. I don't have to know. None of that matters anyway.

What matters is that I can see her right here—even between this ritual breathing—about four feet and a few inches. About fifty, the bright skin on her round face darkened around the raised cheeks. I can see her sweat-slick neck and the hair on her nape glowing in the morning sun. I can see the few strands of white on her neatly brushed black hair flying about her face as she walks around the park in those quirky red shoes, minding her business, nodding at anyone who cares to nod at her. I can see her and hear her speak in that strange dialect to the fellow Chinese who stop to say hello—the music of the rounded vowels—magical even when I play it back in memory, even when I can't understand a word.

When I hear her speak, the strangeness of the words forces the mind to hold on to the sounds—just the sounds—as if they were a phenomenon in nature that will swiftly pass. And in that brief moment, I must take in every syllable of whatever is being spoken and freeze it in time. It's strange trying to recall the stolen sounds. The acute attention it demands just to catch those fleeting sounds—like catching fish with bare hands—to separate them, embed them in the brain like gemstones. And whenever it happens—whenever I'm within earshot of Ju Li speaking her Chinese Hakka in her little red shoes and moving her sweat-slick neck and moving the corner of her lips, wet from the water she frequently drinks—she seems strange.

Yet, the fact that she's right here in front of me—now in this room and also in that familiar park—every day at exactly the same hour of the day, makes all the strangeness disappear. Makes me think, *I know her*. But I also know she's strange. And that works like a torque drill boring into my head, lodging her into my brain like a lotus seed. I can't resist opening her all up even now when the mind should be focused on breathing. In the park, I'm drawn to her by a power beyond any other power I've known—the power of a strange white flower that has broken through the outer casing of the seed, elemental and unforgettable, delicate and simple and utterly mysterious. I know it's temporary. It'll disappear. I become useless in the face of that power, now, as in the park. Watching the precise movements of her hands and enacting them after her—behind closed eyes, under the rising sun—is like an act of resistance, also an act of revival just as potent as mounting plaques on the walls of this history house. And that I know nothing about her makes me determined to keep it that way. I don't want to know. I'd do nothing to change it. Hear no one. Find out nothing.

By the time I'm ready to go out, the flowers have become bone dry in the container. I take the flowers out, one at a time, and place them inside a pink drawstring hemp sack which is perfumed and emptied of all the candy. With the moisture sucked out of them, the flowers look like glass. Brittle. Cold. Sharp-edged. I can hear the dogs again, rabid and waiting in the shadows. I need the umbrella. When was the last time I carried an umbrella to the park? I pull it off the closet hook where it has been left hanging for as long as I can remember. *Does it even work? Is it even strong enough for me to lean on?* I open and shut it once. Then again.

My mind races. The heart races. I feel restless walking down the three flights of stairs, out of my house, onto the street. Today, I'll take a different approach, alter the method slightly, avoid the butcher's where the stray dogs troop this time of the day, smelling the goats being slaughtered, waiting for the blood to roll under the closed door long before they can get a bite of the shavings flung at them. Today, I'll avoid blood. Today, I'll take the scenic route past Onrait First and Best Cycle. No matter if that adds another kilometre both ways. Anything to keep the dogs at bay.

Outside, it's chilly. And it isn't much later than usual. I know I should walk faster. But my knees are slowing me down, or maybe it's the brand-new walkers. I liked my old walkers. But Toshie tossed them out. These walkers feel heavy today. I can feel their weight travelling up my feet towards my chest, like a knife that flashes in and out of the body so fast I can only feel the wound long after. I lose balance, fall to the ground. Did I misjudge my time? Is this racing heart a portent? Will everything end for me here on the street?

A milkman bikes past, stops at a distance, returns to help me onto my feet. I shake him off. *I don't need you. Go away. I'm all right. Would everyone let me be, please?* I squat on the street for a couple of minutes. I know there is still some distance to the park. It sure feels chilly today. It's then that I look up to see the sky. The sky is overcast. I pop an aspirin into my mouth, wash it down with my spit.

Back in the park, Ju Li has already started her Tai Chi with the usual group of players—Hong, Chang, Hao, Liang, Mitra, Lawrence, Rupert, Fu. They stand around her in a circular formation. Like always. I see them every day. But I don't know any of them beyond the half names, just as they know nothing of me except to call me Sen. I break through the inner circle and head straight to Ju Li with the hemp sack dangling from my left hand, umbrella from my right. Without missing a step, without pause, without letting my eyes betray anything too quickly, I look at her no more than a second, transfer the pink hemp sack automatically onto my right hand—the hand of good deeds—and hold it out towards her. Of course, she's startled. Of course, she isn't expecting flowers today. Her perfect eyebrows are cocked with surprise. *What did I get?*

"Pumpkin flowers. For you." I barely manage to blurt it out. My throat is parched. I'm not sure she heard. I repeat. Her face breaks into a smile as I open the hemp sack for her to look inside, to show her what I got. Then I stand watching as her sweaty face shimmers in the sudden burst of sun cutting through the sky. She opens the drawstring on the hemp sack, dips her face into the sack, then pulls out. She draws on the string, closing it. Then she opens it and dips her face into the dark of the sack-mouth again and pulls out again before holding the sack of flowers close to her chest as if meaning to say something with those repeated gestures.

Then she opens the sack once more and dips her hand into it, just to feel the flowers in the dark before bringing a handful out into the open. Now, holding them close to her face, she presses her face into the still-intact halo of the petals. Taking a deep breath, she looks up at the sky. The aspirin worked; the heart is still now; my ears are warm. I can feel the insides of my mouth; the bitterness has slowly washed away. But the moment I start thinking about the heart, it starts to race again. Not the usual way. Not the usual slamming-into-my-chest-like-a-piston-and-staying-stuck-like-a-magnet way. But in a strange way, as though it were shivering in the breeze like a tree branch. I can tell the difference. I haven't felt like this in a long time.

The group of Tai Chi players looks on. They seem to be politely reining in the irritation at what they probably think is much fuss over something quite ordinary. They think nothing of the pumpkin flowers. They've made fritters out of them their own way and crunched them down with tea. Others, who have never in their lives seen pumpkin flowers so grand, come close to Ju Li and take in the scent of the flowers right off her open palm. Eventually, Ju Li drops the flowers back inside the sack. Everyone returns to their places in the circle. I return to my place on the fringe, looking up at Ju Li as she starts her Tai Chi, only to stop again. She opens the sack again and looks inside again, as if to make sure the flowers are still there, before dipping her hand into the sack's dark mouth one more time, feeling them before drawing them out by the handful and holding them close to her face. She puts them back again and, again, draws the string around the hemp sack ever so carefully and, again, takes a deep whiff of the closed sack and looks out to the sky as if to register that smell to her memory. Like a time capsule to be opened in secrecy. She repeats the sequence again. And again. As if she has had enough Tai Chi for the day. As if she's in a trance. And even when the huge fig tree under which we all stand swoops in the face of the strong breeze, and the skies shimmy with thunder, her trance remains unbroken.

They smell just as good as they feel, she seems to gesture with her hands. The Tai Chi players laugh at her, at the banality of the repeating gestures. And they laugh even more as she disregards them and repeats the act as if relishing the irritation caused by the force of her gestures. She doesn't care what they think. And then the clouds break; it begins to rain.

I come up close to Ju Li. I want to ask her out. I've prepared myself all night. To me, she has never appeared stranger. But she gestures at the umbrella. Without a word, I flip it open. Holding on to the sack of flowers in her left hand, my arm with her right, she urges me on, towards the gates on the south end of the park. But that's the wrong way. My usual approach back home is towards the north. I let myself free, following the tow of Ju Li's wet arm. We don't say a word as we walk that unknown path. It feels as if she's still caught up in a trance, and me—fully conscious—I'm flowing along just so as not to nudge her out of it.

She weaves in and out of cramped lanes. We reach the doorway of a brick house with a wood archway painted gold. I've never been to this part of town. A street sign, craggy with dirt and bird shit, points towards the east. I don't know where that street goes. Should I carry on or head back the same way I came? I try to feel the heart; it's there—pumping. I wait for it to slam against my chest. But it doesn't slam. It only shivers, as if it has been restored to a different kind of beat. Ju Li pushes me towards her house. The doorway to the two-storey house is so narrow, I have to fold the umbrella in order for both of us to squeeze through together.

Still holding me by the arm, Ju Li pulls me through the dark hallway on the ground floor. As I walk up the dim corridor, I see shadows wrapped in blankets, still sleeping in the two rooms along the hallway. Now a kettle. I hear it on the stove. It's happening. It's for real. I'm not in a trance. We walk past a stack of shoeboxes, a heap of raw hides, a mountain of dusty paperwork, and Ju Li strides on unmindfully towards the red cement stairway to the east end of the house.

The narrow landing at the top of the stairway spreads out into a whitewashed corridor that runs the entire length of the second floor. Facing the landing is a room with a bright red door and a grilled window. Behind the black iron grillwork of the window, the room is dark. Towards the far left of the corridor where I stand, I can see someone, perhaps house help, mopping the floor. I stand by, watching her. The house help is startled as Ju Li, facing the closed door, pauses for a moment as if to catch her breath, and then, still holding on to my arm, pushes the red doors open with a delicate foot tap.

As I stumble on the raised saddle of the doorframe into the darkness of the room, surrendering to the tug of Ju Li's soft hand around my arm, I pause, trying to catch some air, to gather myself, to make sense of whatever is happening, whatever is about to happen.

As we enter, familiar objects around the room spring out of their contours—the balcony facing the street outside; a bed by a window far up on the left towards the balcony; a worktable on the right; shelves huddled around the table; books inside the shelves; gold letterings on the spine; blue and white porcelain; a wardrobe with a red raincoat and embroidered purple boxes stacked on top of each other.

A checkered morning pours in through the window slats and lines up on the blood-red bed sheet neatly tucked into the mahogany bed frame. Everything in the room, even ashes from burnt incense sticks, seems to have a form, a place of its own. In the far right of the room, towards the balcony, a stone Buddha sits demurely under a red electric lamp inside a carved wood shrine hung up on the wall. A raw sapodilla sits inside a wicker basket at Buddha's folded feet as if set up to ripen in the light.

As I look around, tiny Buddha idols in all shapes and sizes—wood, brass, and porcelain—look back at me in every imaginable posture. It's hard making things out in the dark, but Ju Li doesn't put the lights on. I don't know what she wants.

She strides the length of the room, seats me on the bed—closer to the window on the far side—pushes the window out into the balcony. The damp morning sun rushes in. Blue figurines—gnomes and trolls and angels—stare back from the balcony between rows upon rows of bonsai banyans, mango and fig and jacaranda, bell, bougainvillea, hibiscus, dahlia, and rose-lily. The balcony, which looks like a slap-on afterthought from the street, is something else. A forest. Tiny drops of rain hang from the bonsai like glass beads.

I look around for Ju Li. A moment ago, she was by my side, looking out the window. Now she's back dipping her right hand inside the pink hemp sack, again and again, drawing a handful of bright yellow flowers out of the sack and letting them fall in a brilliant shower near the folded feet of the stone Buddha inside the shrine. Now she's back. I can sense her, smell her breath. As I turn around, Ju Li holds out the hemp sack towards me, her rain-moist eyes gesturing for me to repeat the act.

Outside, it has long stopped raining, but the sky is still overcast. The iron grillwork is shining, as though it has just been sprayed with a fresh coat of paint. I've come a long way to find this place. Now I'm uncertain I'd ever be able to trace my way back home. What time is it? I hear church bells at a distance. My heart has calmed down; I can barely feel it. The stray dogs outside are barking. But they're far away. I can't hear them.

1999

BRAMPTON

⌣AURO

The Lottery

As I look for a spot to park, Milli calls. “I won!” She’s fighting for breath like she won a lottery. I don’t believe a lottery is what we need right now. We’re past all that. I roll down the passenger-side window to look at the person driving the black sedan that steals into the spot I’ve been angling for. As usual, it’s a busy Monday at the liquor store.

But it is a lottery. She won it. It was held at the Mata G. HQ, and Milli has beaten more than two hundred applicants for the right to host her guru at home.

“Will this do it?” I poke her.

Milli is angling to be a trustee at the local chapter of the Mata G. spiritual order. At the dining table, she’s so excited, she isn’t even eating. She uses her knife to dissect the scalloped potatoes on her plate, then she turns on the lettuce and dices it, carefully holding the stalk down with her fork, then she turns to the curried peas. She wants something. I know when she wants something.

“How long is she going to stay?” I watch her face.

“Four nights.” She searches for a reaction.

"What's the problem?"

"The head office says they can't find the old application. You need to turn in a new one."

I don't answer. I know what she's asking—you're all in or nothing; that's how the order works. No place for doubters. Certainly not in the immediate family if you're aspiring to become a trustee. No room for broken families either. Not at the top. That's her pickle.

I had met Mata G. at her ashram in India seven years back, in 1992. When they asked me to complete the *Getting to Know You* form, I knew it was not for me. *What makes you want to be spiritual?*

"It's a natural question," Milli had said.

It has been seven years since I saw my father. I feel I abandoned him since he started seeing this other woman. Guilt is a good place to start. But there is an interview right after, where they hold each word like an egg to the candle, looking for cracks. *Why do you feel you're alone?*

"Because no one loves me, and I love no one." Apparently, that's where they get you're not being truthful. Milli said she had bungled this one, too, but she didn't warn me. She's a teacher at the order. She used to visit Mata G. in Rishikesh every year. Now Mata G.'s spiritual centres have sprung up all over North America. The new centre coming up on Balmoral Drive, Brampton, is ten minutes from where we live. Mata G. is on the last leg of her annual North American tour. The GTA stop has been specially carved out so she can consecrate this new centre—a reclaimed nineteenth-century church that has cost over a million dollars to buy and renovate.

The order here is run by a board of trustees. They work full-time for Mata G. That's what Milli wants to do. She told me this when they invited her to lunch as they started scouting locations for the new centre. They needed her to help organize donations, pitch at various levels of the hierarchy to get their *grand opening* inserted into Mata G.'s Global Events itinerary. Milli isn't on the board yet, but the visit of the guru at her home will do it. She knows. She has worked hard. Will it pay as much as her bank job? We haven't talked. Discussing money makes her angry.

I look at her again, at the wisp of white hair framing the lined face, and I feel sad, not the usual bitterness. When faith blinds someone you care for, what else should you feel? Her lips are parted as if she has been holding something that is gone, like a cigarette stub that has burnt itself out, and she doesn't know.

I remember when the face was firmer, the neat cornrows sweaty in the hot afternoons in Black Creek, where I rented a room in a basement. I was in college. Milli's newly arrived family rented the other room. They had come from a different region in India than me. Milli's family knew Mata G. long before they got here. Long before they got Milli initiated into the order. They pickled dried Bombay duck for canapés. Those days, Milli served them a certain way—after a film we watched together—one canapé at a time, held between the lips as we ate in bed, locked in the lotus position, naked. Then, one day, her parents found out.

I remember having to think really hard about most of the questions in the form. *Were you ever a believer?* What is it that they really want—whether I've believed in something else and had it bad? Or if I'm the sort who's always looking for bad? Or has the bad made me rotten—or ready? Milli says there are no right answers. I made them up anyways. The first time was okay. Must have been. Because I was in.

And we were in love. Meat, alcohol, garlic, onions—it doesn't matter what you give up for that sort of thing. I had no trouble with either sitting in front of a bowl of water and watching myself become a godhead or hallucinating my gradual transformation into a floating lotus. But soon things went sideways, as they always do with hash tokes. I got fat, the sex got affected. I quit.

And now she wants me to do it all over again: Renew the membership. Return to the fold. Revise the answers. Which is way easier, Milli says. But it's quite the opposite because without access to your original answers how the hell does one remember—*your place in the universe, your idea of the self, why you love what you love?* After an interval of seven years, the form is still the same.

Right now, though, watching her peck at the cauliflower, I'm wondering about the other option—chuck it all and get the hell out. But I won't do that. It's not about hope or despair. It might be just a little bit, but not exactly. I don't know how to describe it in words—when you're the wick in the candle burning closest to the base where it's blue-dark and not even hot. That's where I am; that's how it feels. I know she's pretending if she doesn't know it.

"What if the answers match exactly?"

"They'll know you're a liar," Milli blurts out as if she expected the question. But a smirk plays on her lips. "But they'll thank you for not forgetting and thank you for not changing and thank you again for returning."

"What if I remember nothing?"

"You write what you don't remember."

"Why don't you write it for me?"

"Because we don't remember the same things, and I don't want to lie for you." Milli works her knife too hard; a squished chickpea jumps off the plate.

Later, as she brushes her hair after bathing, I come over and grab her from behind.

"Let me do that." I love touching her hair. I know she'll let me do it today.

Milli hesitates, then hands me the comb. "No, not there," she says.

I hold my hand over her eyes before running the wide-toothed comb through her naturally curly, greying hair. And when the comb gets stuck in the frizz, I disengage, take a dab of coconut oil from the jar, and rub it gently into the tangled hair. I use my fingers to run through the length of it, from the roots—where my fingers feel warm and wet—down to the ends, where they feel staticky dry and empty. I press my hand to her eyes again, making sure they're still shut as if asking for a favour—*trust me, I won't hurt you*—but in reality, I can sense it in the way her body stays stiff and uptight. She's being watchful. If one thing goes wrong, she'll pull away.

"If you're both ready to pull away, it must be easy. Right?" Gina, my assistant at work, doesn't get it. She thinks it's about the strength to do right. "You do what you got to do." Not that Gina wasn't ever married. But every marriage is *unique* (another taboo word in the form). And knowing one is not enough. And Milli, in our marriage, works hard to make things look perfect. She has to. She's not going to make it easy. Not for me nor for the trustees of the order of Mata G.

So what now? I'm going to be careful and gentle and tender with her hair until my hands begin to hurt. That's how it is. That's how it has been the past year and the year before that when the doctors told her it'd take a miracle for her to go past the second trimester. We have even stopped trying.

"Just don't say anything stupid when you meet her," she says as I put the comb on the dresser and draw her closer. She resists. Of course, she isn't in the mood. So I hold her from behind, in a mock chokehold, and dig both my thumbs deep into the base of her neck, right above her shoulder blades, into the muscle—holding it there for a minute before running both thumbs down her spine, the left following the right in an ellipsis, stopping at the knot-

Jai looks at the trunk carefully. Then he pulls a claw hammer out of his luggage under the bunk berth and strikes at the lock precisely. The lock splits open. The boy watches as Jai pulls the trunk out into the corridor. It's dark. He throws a wild kick at the light switch and the lights come on, revealing, on one side of the trunk, beautifully patterned layers of silk—sarees stacked tightly. Using his hands, he scours in a frenzy, looking for something as if he knows what he's looking for. Between the silk sarees are other things—a robe, brocaded in gold; daggers inside leather sheaths, scabbed with what look like fake gems; shawls—red, black; white pashmina; blouses made from velvet and taffeta; blouses with trim and frills; rugs with bright rose patterns; rugs with figures, scenes from war; silks threaded with gold and silver; and then a fake crown with a gold patina studded with one large red stone that looks like ruby or tourmaline. Then he finds a pair of black leather straps studded with small metallic bells.

"Whose are these?" Jai holds them up for Veeru to see. He's laughing.

"My mother's," the boy says.

"She was a dancing woman?" Jai winks at me, co-opting me into something.

The boy nods.

"Yeah? You know how to put them on?"

"Yes," the boy says.

"You dance?" Milli asks.

The boy nods.

ted joints. I used to know her joints. I used to know where they knotted up. I used to know where to stop. Milli used to like it this way. She used to want it. But right now, I don't know. She looks unsettled as if she doesn't trust me anymore to hold her from behind, as if she's waiting for something to give in, and then the show will stop.

"If she wants to hold your hand, she'll ask for it," she says. "Don't hold it too tight. Don't just pretend you're there. Be present with her. She doesn't hesitate to let people know she has a temper."

I know why she's still talking today. When I met Mata G. the first time, she had held my hand for what felt like a very long time. I was certain she had drifted off. I had wriggled my hand away. What would you do?

"Don't do that," Milli says.

"Why not."

"Because you're hurting me now."

"How am I hurting you?"

"You're moving your hand in places I don't want."

"What do you want?" There, that's another question in the form.

"Don't always *think* about it. Don't do anything with your hands."

Milli takes off her robe, gets into her side of the bed, and starts reading from the hosting manual they've given her. Then she asks me to pass the water from my side table. In the twelve years we've been married, she's always brought her own water to bed. Her flask is missing today. It's always there by the blue toy bear. I sense she's calling for a truce; she needs me to come around, help her with this visit.

And then we're done? We haven't talked about it. I don't know what she's thinking. Maybe something else is on her mind. Maybe it's the miracle she's waiting for. Does she think that's what she won when she won the lottery? The guru is coming home to give it to her. It's a long shot if that's what she believes. She gives the water back to me. We don't talk.

On the day of Mata G.'s arrival, I get home early and head straight to the airport. The flight from Atlanta is delayed. We wait in the lounge facing the only gate that's letting people out. There is a group waiting with a white bouquet and a welcome banner. There are others in the lounge waiting for other people. It's a long wait before Mata G. walks out in an oversized coat. She appears smaller than how I remember last seeing her. She has a slight stoop around her shoulders. A dark muscular man—presumably an aide—walks behind her, in synchronized steps, like a ceremonial guard. A stumpy, hairy-faced female attendant relieves Mata G. of the passport and other stuff she carries in her small hands. She looks tired.

As she comes closer, the group with the bouquet charges towards her. Mata G. spreads out her arms. Then the aide who has been marching in lock-step says something I can't hear. Everyone falls in line quietly and files past Mata G., bending forward in namaste, as they enter and exit the range of her extended arms. I stand to one side. I don't want to do it. After some time, Mata G. rests her arms by her side, tired. When Milli's turn comes, Mata G. does nothing different to indicate she recognizes her. And when I make no effort to move forward, Milli turns to me. I follow her.

In the next little while, Milli finds her way back to Mata G.'s side. That's where everyone wants to be. The president of the local chapter, who is already rubbing elbows with Mata G., now asks volunteers to follow him to the new location for a night vigil. And as the group moves towards the parking lot, Milli digs her elbow into my ribcage as a signal for me to help the maid carting a trolley loaded with two huge suitcases. They're heavy. It's still twilight outside. Milli gets Mata G. to wrap her arm around Milli's neck as she hoists her into our freshly detailed Ford van. It's busy outside the airport. The maid is in the car. The male attendant-guard has followed others to the vigil.

Outside, the late-evening traffic has thinned out. White jet trails shine in the sun-blanched sky like streamers. Even though it's June, Milli chats about the winter and how it seems to never be gone. Mata G. looks out the window—at cars and pylons and people on the sidewalks—quietly nodding, uninterested, as Milli turns around often to explain. The maid looks out, offering no opinion. Milli pitches her voice high, but I sense a disquiet. She has done everything right. Offered herself completely. Yet she's anxious. Suddenly I feel resentful about that.

"That's one of the many golf clubs in this area." Milli points as Mata G. and her maid look out. "And those woods there, they stretch to the Heart Lake Conservation." They're not interested. Suddenly it's eerily quiet inside the car. "We get all kinds of birds this time of year."

"We can go birdwatching if you want," I add. Mata G. doesn't respond. I look at the mirror. She's tired. Milli quietly digs her elbow into my ribs again. Perhaps I spoke out of turn.

Upon reaching home, Milli gets busy laying out dinner. She knows what to serve and in what order. She has studied the handouts. When Mata G. returns from the bathroom, the maid says they've already eaten. All they want now is a place to pray. The evening seems to be finally ending.

"Do you have a prayer room?" the attendant asks me. She's friendlier now.

Before I can reply, Milli stops what she's doing, turns around. "Can you help her with that," she tells me, pointing at a canvas bag. It carries ritual objects needed during prayers. As we walk down to the basement, the attendant says her name is Gowrie. She has been in the order since she was six years old. She says she was hand-picked by Mata G. at sixteen to be her assistant. She has seen the world.

Milli has been working in the basement for the past week, converting a sweaty rec room to a prayer space suitable for a congregation. If she makes trustee, there will be prayer meetings and visitors. She has stood up a makeshift altar against the recessed wall where we used to keep the large flat screen. A hand-crafted wooden *om* wall decor with rustic bells, about two feet in diameter, has been nailed to the wall. It's bracketed by two regular-sized redwood doors that reach from floor to ceiling, giving the place a kind of strangeness that is sacred and ominous. Mats and meditation chairs are placed neatly in a wide semicircle facing the altar. Mata G. seems absorbed in thoughts, but Gowrie looks around, pleased.

The night presses against the window to the left. Under the window, an assortment of Mata G.'s images in dark museum frames of various sizes are hooked to the wall in a zigzag arrangement. The polished parquet at the centre of the floor reflects pot lights from the ceiling. Mata G. sits in half-lotus with her back to the red-door altar. When she sees Milli on her haunches facing her, she gestures for her to sit closer, by her right side, Gowrie is on her left. After a brief chant of *om*, Gowrie produces a portable stereo from the canvas bag and plays the evening prayer track. Mata G's, Gowrie's, and Milli's lips move as they repeat the chanting under their breath, then they start swaying to the chant, then they're in a trance.

When the prayer track ends, Mata G. looks sideways at Milli, grabs her hand, holding it for a long time. Then they start swaying together as if their bodies have merged, as if they can both hear something no one else can. I look at Gowrie. Her eyes are closed. There is a gap between her body and Mata G.'s, yet she seems to be in that magical field; aware of what's happening, she sways alone to the same unheard tune.

And then the swaying stops. Mata G. takes a deep breath, uncouples herself from Milli, rubs her palms together, and runs them down her face. So do my wife and Gowrie. The pre-sleep communion ends.

On her way to the bedroom, Mata G. stops by another photo gallery along the stairway. It's clear Milli has gone overboard with these—monochrome images of the guru in diverse frames arranged like a circle of squares.

"Where did you find these?" Gowrie asks, her face flushed. "I've not seen them anywhere else."

"I blanched the colour off the prints," Milli says.

"These are even better than the original."

"That's because in black and white you can play with the shades of grey whereas in colour you've too many distractions," I say, and Milli looks at me as though I shouldn't have.

"The chronology is wrong," Mata G. says. "Look, it's going backward before going forward." Walking up the stairs, she points at a twenty-year-old picture followed by a forty-year-old and then a picture when she must have been sixteen or seventeen. "But we move in circles, don't we, so it's alright."

It is almost ten. Mata G. wants to get to bed immediately. Milli has it covered. She has read the host manual and memorized everything about Mata G.'s sleep rituals. She likes having her maid available to her at all times. The master bedroom is the only one large enough to accommodate an extra single bed. Milli has surrendered that room. Mata G. will take the king. But the mattress is a bit too high. She needs help climbing onto it. "What if I roll over? I'll sleep here." Mata G. points at the floor.

A round of nervous commotion follows as Milli rushes in and out of the other rooms, dragging quilts and sheets from closets. With Gowrie's help, she lays out the cushions and sheets on the wooden floor. Everything calms down eventually.

Downstairs, I pour myself a tall whisky and wait by the living room window for the raccoons. It's past eleven. The raccoons show up as usual, jump into the trash carts along the length of the crescent. They're gone for the time being. Even though it's garbage day, I haven't put out the trash. Milli doesn't want Mata G. to see trash first thing in the morning. In their Book, it's considered an ill omen.

I drink the remainder of the whisky, rinse the cup, and take the stairs towards the smaller of the two guest rooms Milli has kept for our use. It seems the larger guest room has been readied for the male aide who is spending the night in vigil at the new centre. It'll be used tomorrow, I presume. For some reason, Milli always refers to the spare rooms as guest rooms even though we haven't had any guests since Milli's parents lived with us several years earlier, to help her through the early months of another pregnancy before the chromosome count came out wrong again. We wouldn't have guests again anytime soon.

When I don't find Milli in bed, I look for her in the bathroom. I figure she must still be with Mata G. It seems strange because Milli is an early sleeper. Are they still fussing over beds? I want to know. Avoiding the creaky boards on the hardwood Milli has carefully marked, I slide up close to the master bedroom, press my ears against the doors. Nothing. I notice my own shadow, switch off the hallway lights, and lean in. The door to the bedroom opens.

Inside Mata G. is sprawled on the floor mattress, her face buried in the pillow as if on a masseur's table, her arms flanked out, her dark body interrupted by a towel placed in the middle. Gowrie, seated near Mata G.'s feet, massages her toes. Milli, on her haunches, is by Mata G.'s head. She pours something into her cupped palm before driving her shiny fingers into the roots of Mata G.'s hair, brushed backward from the nape and splayed out on the white of the pillowcase. Light filtering in through the window sheers hovers over Mata G.'s dark skin.

I stand at the doorway. I take in whatever I can as Milli sways backward and forward in a trance-like rocking movement, just as in the prayer room, leaning over to reach the depth of Mata G.'s hair and then sliding down her spine, down to the small of her back, where the towel lies still, crooked. Milli seems to be feeling for knots as she kneads the muscles. It's dark, but for the lighted sheer. Neither of them notices me. A fruity scent hangs over the bedroom before Gowrie raises her head towards the door, just for a moment, before returning to her trance—swaying backward and forward, digging into the arches of Mata G.'s feet. I move away from the door, keep watching until Gowrie looks up again as if she knows I'm there. She can see me. Yet she returns to her trance-like see-sawing.

Embarrassed, I rush downstairs, grab the freshly rinsed mug from the closet and pour another drink. A tall whisky. Over the next hour, I drink up the whole bottle before realizing I haven't eaten. I pour some more and move closer to the window again. I can barely move. My eyes are heavy. It's quiet out and drizzling. The raccoons are gone. There is no moon, but the streetlights drip in a brilliant golden-yellow stream down the roof across the street. A light mist has fallen. Amazing how quickly the weather has changed.

Milli doesn't come to bed all night. In the morning, when I hear her voice, I feel relief. She's chatting with Gowrie about the houseplants that have taken half our kitchen. I remember how Milli's collection started with the prayer plant that the previous owner had left for dead. She brought it back to life—one leaf at a time—and then she added a pinstripe to her collection and a rattlesnake, then a button fern and a golden goddess, and then the whale fin snake plant I got for her fortieth birthday. That was eleven months ago, when we last made love.

When I come down to the dining area, Mata G. is done with breakfast. They're in the middle of a tea ceremony, holding the teacups between their palms, eyes closed, *feeling the warmth of the universe enter and flow out of their bodies.*

Mata G. is dressed in a plain white saree, her hair pulled back in a knotted bun that hangs tightly over her neck.

As I walk into the kitchen, Milli pulls me aside. She says she can smell the whisky on my breath. And why am I up all night drinking at home when it was decided I'll keep it outside? "There is no time for breakfast," she says as I look in the refrigerator. They have to be at the centre by seven-thirty. We head out the door without another word. Milli is nervous. Perhaps she didn't sleep well. Perhaps she's worried. I know she's struggling to look composed.

"On a normal day it takes less than five minutes,' Milli explains as we drive up to the new centre. It takes longer today because the garbage trucks are out. I choose a detour through the school zone and have to stop twice to let school buses off board. I hear Milli complain about the trucks, about the buses, about the kids who don't care to look where they're walking.

As the lotus dome of the new centre shows up, a damp after-rain chill filters through the vents in the car. Gowrie helps Mata G. put on a sweater. Then we pull into the parking lot. A group of congregants is already waiting. Milli asks me to park at a distance so Mata G. can get out of the van in her own time, away from the crowd. But Mata G. doesn't want to walk. She prefers to get closer to the main entrance, even if that means she'll have to climb out of the car right into the crowd.

I get off the driveway, onto the grass. The rain has softened the dirt. I try to get Mata G. as close to the entrance as possible. When the car comes to a standstill, a crowd gathers. Someone brings out an ornate throne chair, opens the door and literally scoops Mata G. from the car seat onto the throne. Then they carry her on their shoulders. Maybe Milli didn't know about this nuance. She's outpaced by the rapidly unravelling takeover. She takes a minute to gain composure as Mata G. is reclaimed by the crowd. Gowrie disappears, too. Milli turns as she walks away, waving her phone vigorously to indicate that she'd be calling soon.

As I pull out onto the highway, my throat feels dry, and the left side of my head is heavy as if I had put it inside a freezer. A searing pain burns down my spine. It has happened before. I know it happens whenever I haven't eaten for some time.

On my way to work, I grab a smoked turkey club and a double expresso from the bakery, my regular breakfast haunt. To the usual menu, I want to add something more. Perhaps something sweet. I'm hungry for sugar. I feel I've earned it. I look at the display and point to the yellow tart. I know the egg will make me sick. I know the sugar could kill me. But I've my insulin pen. I'm carrying my anti-allergens. I'm going to have that. And that. And that. One of each.

It's past ten. I'm late for work. It has started raining again. Thankfully, no one has called for me yet. I check my phone and realize I had turned it off the previous night. I turn it back on—missed calls, missed messages float up the small screen. The world has moved, and I wasn't even watching. The store clerk asks if my order is to go, and I consider before deciding I'll skip work. "For here," I say.

The store isn't busy. Everyone is ordering to go. I find a seat in the corner. I notice Milli has called a couple of times. She wants a new mattress for the master bedroom. I think about it for a second and decide to ignore it. I finish the sandwich. Then I unwrap the yellow tart, letting the chilled sweetness drip into my mouth as I bite into the baked egg caramel, listen in to the music of the crisp pastry crumbling inside my mouth. I will have one more, I don't care. I get another of the same. Then I turn to the other stuff on my table—an explosion of cream and colour. I don't feel like returning home. I don't feel like going anywhere, doing anything except sitting still to eat. Watching the world go by.

Then my assistant, Gina, texts me from work. *Missing you*, she says.

Running late, I text back. I finish the tart. The sweetness irritates me now. As I rinse my mouth with the remainder of the coffee, my phone buzzes. Milli again—memory foam. Eight inches. I'm not going to do it. I get everything packed.

Back at work, I do nothing except stare blankly at the computer screen. I don't want to meet anyone. Gina shares her pasta as usual. She says it's the garlic that makes it taste so good—her mother's recipe. Later, I call the store and arrange for an afternoon delivery of the mattress Milli wants. On my way home, I stop over at the usual bar and order the usual extra-large bourbon on the rocks with a twist. Then I have a second. Then a third.

By the time I return to Balmoral, it's past nine. The inauguration ceremonies are over, everyone's gone. I park close to the only other car in the driveway. Sure, it's a bit later than I had intended. I pop a piece of gum in my mouth. For a second, I regret returning there. I make sure I carry my completed form. Milli will need that now.

As I enter, I find Milli and Gowrie and another woman I remember seeing at the airport last night. They sit listening intently as Mata G.'s night-vigil aide explains something with an animated flurry of hands. A few seats away, another man is watching the group, nodding quietly to the night-vigil aide's hand gestures. He seems to be excluded from the conversation but allowed to listen in from the fringe. He strains to listen in. He doesn't want to miss a word. Every sinew of his face is intense. He's tall. I recall he had carried Mata G. on his shoulder this morning.

They seem to be discussing something important. But I'm tired. I don't want to interrupt. I grab a seat closest to the exit, several rows behind the other man. I notice Milli watching me before she breaks away from the huddle and strides the length of the granite hallway, looking at the floor. She's angry. She wants no eye contact. I hand her the completed form. She looks at it briefly, then she asks me to wait outside in the car.

"Is there anything to eat?"

"What?" Milli crinkles her nose before turning back to her place in the huddle. I head out. Even the radio today is annoying—a crazy caller is back again asking for the same song to be played every year, the day he had proposed to his wife, long dead. Why?

Then I see Milli coming out alone, holding the form I just handed her. I know something is wrong. "Mata G. has chosen to stay the night with another family," she says.

"What about us?"

"What about *us*?" She stares as though she's expecting *me* to have an answer.

"What about her stuff?"

"They'll have it moved tomorrow."

"And the lottery? Didn't they say you won it—all four days?"

"Shut up and drive."

I look at her in the dark. I do as she says. Another word and I know she'll crumble. *Did we screw up?* I want to ask when we're closer to home. If there has to be another war, better be done with it now. I don't. Milli says nothing. Did Gowrie see me after all? I don't care.

Back home, the mattress is heavy. I struggle to drag it inside the house. Milli heads straight to the bedroom. I wait downstairs and pour myself a drink. I look out at the dark blue light filtering through the window. The clouds that had strangled the sky all day have begun to clear, revealing the sharp contours of a sickly moon. The green trash cart of the neighbour across the street faces down on the curb. I don't look for the raccoons today. I've been watching the night through this window long enough to know they wouldn't be out today.

After a while, I'm upstairs. Milli is sprawled on the bed, her face buried in the pillow; the silk saree she'd worn to the ceremony coiled like moulted snakeskin by the foot of the bed. I hang around for a minute watching Milli, unsure if I should leave her alone.

Then I walk up to the edge of the bed, fold the saree, hang it in the closet. Seated by the bed, I touch her shoulder, expecting her to yell back, push me away. If she does that, I'll stop. Get another drink. I feel like it. I want to talk; she seems spent. I can feel her muscles responding to the pressure of my fingers. As I move my hands, she adjusts her body into the mattress, letting out a grunt, relaxing her shoulder blades just a little. I take a chance, run my fingers through her hair, pushing it back onto the pillow exactly as I'd seen her do last night on Mata G. I see the magic jar on the nightstand. I pour from it onto my palm—it's just coconut oil. I rub it into Milli's hair—staticky dry and frizzy again—and keep repeating until her naturally curled grey hair stands up glazed like ridges of the cornfields we used to watch, once upon a time, out of her apartment window in Black Creek.

Digging my thumb into the base of her skull, I move my fingers in circles, zippering them down her spine, on top of her nightgown, smudging the soft white cotton with oil. I pull her nightgown away from her bottom and knead the knotted tissue. Then I turn to the muscles of her back, up the length of her spine and then down again, past the buttocks, past the hips and calves, the ankle, down to the toes and the webbing between her toes, feeling for the knots, untangling the frayed nerve ends, polishing her dark golden skin with the oil on my hands.

Milli has fallen asleep. I pull the sheets over her. I feel like another drink. A tall whisky on the rocks. But my feet are heavy. I fold up on the bed beside her. In the haze from the lighted window sheer, she looks exactly like Mata G. herself. And I feel something I haven't felt before. Not pity or guilt or sympathy. Not the hollow feeling I had when I was trying to remember my answers to the questions in the form: *Where were you before you got here? What happens when you die?* Something else. Something hovering between admiration and disgust. I can't describe it in words.

2006

BRAMPTON

KAL

How About a Dragon

I start today at Toshie Sen's as caregiver on the day shift. The boy who gets the door stares at me as if he's expecting someone else. Then he heads back to the woman on the bed.

"They killed her and got rid of the body," the woman says, ignoring me.

Toshie is a cousin. We have hardly met. My mother and Toshie's mother are sisters at war. "It's complicated," is what my sister, Snelly, told me. "The usual family shit."

My guidance counselor says family won't count for the forty hours of community work I need to graduate high school. But Snelly says, "Before wasting four years in a med program, you need to know you can handle it." No one in our family is a doctor, so it's on me.

Snelly says Aunt Rita's dementia isn't real, just a side effect of drugs and depression. "Try to get her to draw."

"It's got to be half the minimum wage, at least," I tell Snelly. She's doing all the talking with Toshie. She understands. "It's a detached red-brick house right by the fire hydrant. You cannot miss it."

Well, not if it's tiny and hidden behind long grass in a yard that hasn't been cleaned in a year. Besides, I've never been this far out west of Brampton. Everything in Brampton feels different.

"They didn't kill her," the boy says, trying to impress me as I pull my brand-new scrubs out of the tote bag. "You can use my dad's room to change." I notice the boy speaks slowly, as if he's fighting a lisp. He must be ten or eleven.

"Just yesterday she was there. Now it's someone else doing the same part." Aunt Rita looks distracted. Her voice trails off as if she has lost interest even before the words get out of her mouth.

"Mom said they replace actors who stop working hard." The boy knows Aunt Rita is watching me. He gently touches her before explaining. His brown eyes are fixated on her.

"Who's this?" the woman asks. "Shut the TV," she says. "It's hurting my eyes."

It's ten after nine, the last week of June. The sun presses in through the basement window, taking the air in a chokehold. The boy sits on the bed for a while, cupping Aunt Rita's discarded hearing device to make it squeal, then he leaves the room. Then he calls someone and whispers on his phone.

Aunt Rita looks like she hasn't eaten for days. She has an oval face and a high forehead. She must have been gorgeous once. But her chiselled features are sallow now, and her whip-thin frame under the extra loose gown makes her look spooky and gaunt. Her ungroomed hair has patches of grey, and she has only one eye open—her right eye—blank and huge as it tapers to the outer edge like a ripped blue petal. A perfect scar runs the length of her thick eyebrow like the spine of a blackfish.

"Come here," the woman yells out as if she wants to look me up closely.

By then the boy has walked out to the kitchen and is jamming a slice of bread. The boy wears shorts and a red sweatshirt over his loopy shoulders. He has a shock of black curly hair that overruns his small face. It's so hot, I can feel my arms sticking around the armpits. The AC is on. It makes the sound of a meat grinder, starting and stopping frequently, doing nothing to the heat. A familiar curry smell sits like an overlay in the entire apartment.

The sudden yelling startles the boy. He drops the bread. It falls on the side of the jam. He scrapes the jam out of the tiles, cleans the floor with a wet towel, gets himself another slice of bread from the fridge and puts another sloppy layer back on. From his careful actions, it seems the boy is used to being alone, but he's worried about the lost bread. He pushes it down in the trash; he doesn't want it found.

I walk to the kitchen and ask in a low voice, "What grade are you in?"

"Six." The boy chomps rapidly. "I'm not supposed to eat this."

"Why not."

"I just had breakfast. But I'm already hungry." He's about five feet, but layers of fat pleated up his waist make him look shorter. "Do you want some?" The boy's hairy face has broken out.

"I've already eaten," I say.

"Switch off the TV. Will you?" Aunt Rita cranes her neck, searching for the boy.

"Mom asked me to keep it on." The boy moves back from the kitchen into his area—half of a large living room—separated by a sliding Plexiglas partition. His half is fitted with a bed, a chair, and a table, facing a wall closet with both doors taken out.

"How would she know?" Aunt Rita speaks in a hushed tone.

The boy walks over to the bed. "Look at the camera there." He stares at her, anticipating a reaction. "She can see everything."

"Is she even my daughter . . . or police?"

"Are you going to eat breakfast now?" he asks.

"How many daughters do I have?"

"That one." The boy waits, before adding, "And I'm your grandson. And that man there is your husband." The boy points at a young man in an army hat and uniform in the photo. Then he walks over to his half of the room. I watch the boy as he moves from one side to the other. Like a yo-yo, tethered to his computer, where he's playing a game. The woman stays curled on the bed, clinging to her pillow. For a long time, she remains still, staring at the white-hot sky pressed against the basement window. Then she wakes up with a start as her bed shakes, and the AC starts grinding again.

"There, someone just broke in."

"Would you like to draw?" I try to distract her from the noise.

"Can you check upstairs?" She cranes her neck towards the stairway.

"Don't worry about upstairs," the boy says, pounding his keyboard.

The woman doesn't hear him. She stares at the ceiling, still trying to make out the sounds.

"Can you find out?" she whispers, cocking the good eyebrow. "What day is it?"

"Thursday," I say and leave the room. Out in the hallway, it's darker; the lights have all been switched off. I walk up to the stairway leading upstairs. I hear people shuffling, floorboards creaking, voices yelling at each other. I try to listen in, but the AC drowns out everything. The door leading up is chain locked.

"I don't see anyone," I say. "Let's do breakfast and after that, we could try something new."

"Who was that?" the woman stares.

"The door is locked."

"Go check again. I want to go home." The woman's face shakes as she raises her head and yells, "What's your name?"

"Kal," I say.

"What sort of a name is that?"

"Never mind her." The boy makes a funny chortling sound; he's embarrassed.

"I want to go home. Did you hear that?"

"Do you miss home?" I ask. *Talk about feelings*, I read it in the caregiver's manual. "Do you remember how it was? Would you like to draw it?" I realize she isn't wearing her listening device.

"The boy has the key. Go up and check. No one's going to pay you for sitting here, staring up my face. You understand? I need to go home."

I walk over to the other side where the boy is still pounding his keyboard. Leaning in close, I whisper, "Who lives upstairs?"

"Upstairs is rented. It has been several years. She thinks I'm lying."

"Why is the door chained?"

"Because she wanders off. Once she fell down those stairs," the boy says, facing his computer, working his mouse, punching randomly on the keyboard, consumed by the fantasy unfolding on his screen.

When he realizes I'm watching, he pauses the game, stands up, and stomps the parquet floor close to his feet as if by doing that, he can fool Aunt Rita into believing her words have been acted on. I watch the boy. He smiles. Just then the doorbell rings.

"I'll take it," I say. I'm finding it hard just to stand still. How am I going to last the day?

"Who is that?" The woman crawls out of bed, coming after me, but stops abruptly near the camera.

"Someone was asking if we need the grass cut." I guide the woman back to the bed. "Would you like to do some work?"

"Who asked you to open the door?"

"There is a package outside. Would you like me to drag it in?"

"That's my mom's beauty stuff," the boy says. He seems to have half his ear on whatever is going on on the other side between me and Aunt Rita.

"That's a huge box." I try not to sound curious.

"She sells them," the boy says.

"Did the courier leave?" the woman yells out from her bed. "What about my things? When will they get that?"

"Do you need a bathroom break?" I reach out and grab Aunt Rita's arm, trying to steady her as she prepares to get off the bed—kicking the sheets around her feet and pushing herself to the edge, she slides her body off the bed frame.

"I want to go home." She walks up to the door and stops again right under the camera. "Someone has broken in. Can you check?" the woman orders the boy. The boy is still facing away, pounding his keyboard. He pretends not to have heard her.

When he doesn't reply, she tries to rush over to his half of the room, misjudging the partition on the left—the side of her bad eye—and trips. I didn't expect her to move that fast. I'm right beside her, but I'm slow to react. Aunt Rita snatches my hand, balancing herself before digging her nails into my wrist and twisting hard.

I snatch my hand back. Then I move away, just as the manual says. "Fuck me. What the hell are you doing?" I scream out loud, not from pain. I'm frustrated. I can't help it. The boy turns around. His face is red—from terror or anger or embarrassment, I can't tell. The woman goes back to her bed as soon as the boy turns, and his eyes meet hers. A blue patch forms around my wrist.

"Put an ice pack," the boy says, returning impassively to the game as if it has happened before. "There's ice in the fridge. You can grab a towel from the washroom."

After a while, the blue mark darkens. The AC comes back on again. I look at my wrist. Numb. I want to leave before I lose my cool again and blow it. The boy sees I haven't moved. He gets up and returns with the ice and rolls it on my hand.

"She becomes cranky anytime she sees a stranger," he explains. "What would you like her to draw?"

"Actually, I think I should leave."

The boy keeps rolling the ice. More than the pain or the blue hurt, what's bothering me is that I yelled at the woman on camera, and everyone is going to know.

"I've drawing paper," the boy says. "You can use my crayons if you like." He touches the blue spot on my wrist with his moist fingers and blows on it. And then he starts massaging the ice around the hurt again.

The woman, now leaned back on the bed, avoids looking at us. Then she starts mumbling—the same sounds over and over as though she realizes something isn't fitting in right, and she can fill in the blanks with repetition.

After some time, she becomes still as if she has entered a trance, looking at the window near the ceiling. Her left eye—like a scar—permanently shut off by pleated skin. Her good eye—droopy as if it weren't her own—straining to see through the stained window, through the particles of dust that hang like shards of glass in the sun blazing through the stained well cover. Then she starts moving her lips again, blinking rapidly.

Toshie had given me the list of meds. It seems the effect of opiates from last night has worn off. After a while, she waves at the boy, and as he comes closer, she says her throat feels like something is stuck inside.

"I'll get you water." The boy moonwalks to the kitchen.

"What's in there?" The woman points at my tote bag on the sofa.

"Food," I say.

The boy fetches the tote bag, opens it up for the woman to look inside. "Drawing board, paper, wax pastels," he explains. "I've never seen her draw." He cups his mouth to whisper, even as he holds a glass of water to her mouth. The woman sips like a child, taking frequent breaks, making no effort to stop as water seeps past the corner lines, then down her furrowed face. Then she drifts off looking at the soundless images on the TV forming and unforming.

By the time the woman wakes up, I must have called my cousin Toshie twenty times. I've called my sister's work. Someone needs to tell me it's okay to leave.

The woman starts mumbling again, carefully inspecting

her own forearm. "It's a man's hand. Someone is twisting a scooper in my eye. Get the hell off me. Why doesn't the hand stop?"

My phone rings briefly and disconnects as I try to answer. I see Toshie's number flash on the screen.

"Who's that?" The woman is distracted again. Then she starts raising herself on the bed, looking for something to hold on to. I call Toshie again. She doesn't answer.

"Who are you calling?" the woman asks.

"I'm calling your daughter."

"Show me the phone." The woman gets off the bed, wobbles.

I hand her the phone. It's a brand-new Telstra Hiptop 2. She looks at the screen, tries to figure out the buttons, then she gives up.

"Do you have another number for your mom?" I ask the boy.

"Why? What did I do? What do you want to say?"

After that, something strange happens to the woman's face. Perhaps the mention of her daughter. Her eyes flash. She seems to remember something. Her face hardens. Her jaws tighten and her fingers, pressed around my phone, shake as if she's trying to draw strength from a faraway place. Her body jangles as if she has lost control of her nerves; blood rushes to her face. She looks out to the stained well cover at the sound of something cracking; it's a blue-tailed bird pecking at the well cover, trying to break it open. She cocks her body in the shape of a discus thrower and tosses the phone towards the bird as if she wants to knock the bird's head with that strike. The phone hits the tiled drywall ceiling, then the window, then it crashes onto the corner of the footboard, face down. The screen explodes.

The boy walks over and grabs the phone. It looks like someone has hammered a rivet into the screen. "I'll tell Mom. She can see on the camera what happened. She'll have it fixed. You can use mine." He offers an old flip phone.

"No." The woman raises herself on the bed, yelling again. "Don't give it to him." For some reason, she's shivering as though she's getting chills, or she's fighting an invisible force wrestling her. "You're not here to play on the phone," she pants, barely able to speak. "I'll throw you out if I see you on the phone again." Then she pauses to regain her breath. "It's time for my breakfast. Go get me some tea first."

The kitchen stove is crammed with blue casserole pans covered with glass lids. I see scrambled eggs, hash browns, and gravy. The sides of the pans and the metal cooktop are smudged with traces of food as if someone has scooped the contents of the pans in a rush. The food is cold. I need to move the casserole dishes before I can turn the burner on. I don't know if I should be touching any of that. I realize the boy is behind me, breathing heavily. "Could you move them off?"

"Mom said we should use the microwave."

I stand there for a second. I don't think I can do this

anymore. I've never brewed tea in a microwave. I feel like tossing a spoon and blowing it. It hasn't been a week since I got the new phone. Someone would have to pay for this.

The boy starts showing me the settings on the microwave. I'm not interested. I've picked up a teaspoon, plotting my next move before he stares at me and stops talking. I can't stand him anymore. I'm panting again. The boy gently steps in, takes over. Holding a stained carafe under the tap, he fills it to the 3-cup mark, then he puts two tea bags into the carafe and places it in the microwave. Then he pours the steaming red liquid into two cups. Then he walks over to a closed wood cabinet and whisks out a bottle of brandy.

"This will calm her down before Dad gets her prescription." He pours the brandy straight out of the bottle into one of the cups, then puts the bottle back in the cabinet. In the other cup, he scoops three spoons of sugar and a dollop of cream. "Do you want tea?" he asks me as I run my finger across the broken phone. I want to be out of there. My head hurts so badly, I'm sure it's about to explode. I didn't expect things to fall apart so quickly. I dash off to the washroom.

By the time I return, the boy is slurping on his milky tea. He has brought the breakfast onto the bed. Sitting by the woman, he gently strokes her exposed leg as if begging her to get up and eat. But he can't make her eat. She has folded up on the bed, holding herself tenderly. I wait in the hallway watching the boy. He gives up after some time and returns the untouched food to the casserole. I realize my own stomach has started growling. It's almost noon. I've got a bowl of pasta in my bag, but I don't want to eat it cold. I don't want to get close to the microwave either.

I look around. The walls of the room are covered with photos in thin-rimmed frames. In one of the pictures, I see the woman, much younger, playing in the rain with her children. I can't make out the place. In another picture, she's serious, wearing dark glasses beside an older man with a walrus moustache.

"That's my grandpa," the boy says.

I don't answer. I stay in the hallway, refusing to get back into the sick room. If I leave now, they'll say I'm unreliable; if I leave after three hours, they'll say I'm a quitter. I shouldn't have taken this gig.

On the bed, the woman seems to be drifting in and out of sleep, muttering under her breath. I go around her bed and look for the plug on the wall socket that the boy says connects the camera to Toshie's phone. I find it, yank it out. Perhaps this will make Toshie call me back. There is no way I'm going to continue at half the minimum wage if it involves violence.

After some time, the boy walks over to me. "She won't bother you for a while. You can eat now if you want. There's stuff in the fridge, too." He opens the fridge and shows me.

I don't answer. Something about the boy tells me if I walk out right now, he wouldn't understand. Perhaps it's his large hairy head, his rabbit ears. Perhaps it's the way he moves between the sick room and his own little hole in the closet. Like a yo-yo. Or maybe not like a yo-yo but like a pendulum keeping time. He seems to be in control.

"Who's winning?" I ask as he returns to his computer. I watch him move pixelated blocks on his screen—like a pro—building and breaking things as he likes, firing at zombies that pop up at random. I know what he's doing. I don't play that game anymore.

"It took me two hours to build this, and now I'm stuck."

"Who are you playing?" I know he isn't playing anyone.

"Can we do the drawing?" he asks.

"It's for her to do."

"How would anyone know?"

"Well, you have the camera, don't you?" I point to the wall.

"Not anymore. You took it down, didn't you?" He smiles wryly like someone who accidentally revealed a secret.

"Do you want to plug it back in?"

"Mom is busy today. She isn't watching. How about a dragon?"

"What about it?"

"I can draw a dragon, if you like."

A dragon is fine. At least it'll take my mind off the clock. I pull out the white construction sheets and wax pastels from my tote bag. He holds the sheet vertically, draws a V, turns it over to landscape. "That's the mouth." Then he draws the body, jaws, legs, and claws. He takes his time to do the belly, carefully connecting the outer and inner body with perfectly straight lines, then he adds the horns and teeth. When it's time to do the eye, he breaks form, draws it large, like a cyclops, covering the entire head. Then he makes the back spikes, adds the fire. He breathes heavily as he draws. His ears turn red.

I stand and watch as he sketches out the last of the back spikes. Then he draws another dragon with a slightly smaller tail, smaller everything—smaller spikes, smaller legs and arms—but he makes the V of the mouth larger, as if it were smiling without teeth—defanged of menace—and without fire. Then he draws another with an even smaller body and horns and spikes, smaller eye. And then the fourth dragon, smaller than the previous. "We can have her colour them all."

"What colours would she need?"

"Black for the big dragon, red, blue, yellow for the others."

"Why did you make four?"

"We can cut them out and make them fight."

"What's in the loot chest?"

"Fight or die, like the heroes in our True Legends class. The black dragon lives underground with three others, all white, but they can change colours, at will, to blue or red or yellow. Nothing can stand on the ground above them because someone is stealing the builders' tools and knocking over walls. It's the black dragon shaking everything down after the builders leave. But not all of them are as bad. And no one knows that. Because no one can reach that deep where the dragons live. To build a castle, you have to have the dragons come out of the hole. Night attracts dragons and light will kill the BIG one. He doesn't know that yet. Someone has to keep him awake."

"What will happen after BIG is dead?"

"The other dragons will get a piece of the castle and live happily ever after." His ears have become red again. I gently touch his shoulder. Then I touch his head. Then I start moving my fingers in small circles against the sinew of his curly hair. I don't know what I'm doing. I feel like calming the boy. My hands move automatically.

He sits still for a while before bursting out in a nervous chuckle, shaking me off. I stand by, watching him colour the dragons exactly as he said—black for the BIG, blue for the slightly smaller, then red, yellow . . . before I hear something crashing—the sound of metal hitting wood, then the sound of metal slapping water.

As I walk to the other side, I notice the woman has set herself up on the edge of the bed again and is dangling her legs while her soak-wet gown leaks onto a pool of urine on the floor. The bed pan is upturned, the urine slowly spreads out, takes over the entire apartment. I stand still, clueless as ever, trying to recall from the caregiver's manual. I stare at the woman, hating her.

"Look at what you did," the woman says, terrified, searching my eyes before the corners of her good eye explode into an impish smile.

The boy comes over from the other side. He seems to know what has happened. Perhaps such a thing has happened before because he's quick to turn around. Without another word, he fetches a mop and a bucket from somewhere and is down on his haunches soaking up the mess. I feel sorry watching him. I rush to the washroom and splash my face. When I return, I find the boy on the bed rubbing the woman's back, softly whispering into her ear, while she sits like a trapped animal, terrified.

"Where did you go?" the woman asks me and keeps repeating the question as she and the boy sit like that, locked into each other, doing nothing. Then the boy goes down to the floor again and moves around in small, measured steps—just as he was moving on his computer screen a little while ago—holding the red steel pole, swinging the mop head, left then right, in a perfect arc before wringing the wet mop back into the dispenser, all in one action as if it was another game. Then the doorbell rings. The boy and the woman exchange a quick glance. The boy stops.

It's the boy's father. He's a dark, no-neck man about forty. Black hair on his large head has receded to the point where it sits like a halo. Walking into the room, he squinches at the odour.

"Why didn't you put on the diaper?" he asks me. "Did no one tell you she needs to be taken to the washroom every hour? Did she eat anything?" He doesn't pause for me to answer.

I say I don't remember. I don't want to lie about the brandy. I don't know if the truth would hurt the boy. The smell of urine seems to be getting on the man's nerves. He puts the mop bucket away, pulls out a disinfectant spray from a drawer in the woman's room, and sprays every corner of the apartment. The smell of the disinfectant is so strong, I almost choke, rush to the washroom again—my fourth visit since I started. I don't think I can handle it. I want to stay in the washroom if I can.

And I must have stayed there long because when I return to the sick room, I find the man has changed out of his security uniform into shorts and a T-shirt and has settled at the small table by the kitchen, eating.

"I got the prescription," he says. "Here. You can give it to her right now." And without pausing, "Give it to her with something warm. Make her some hot tea. Not black. I just got chamomile. It's on the fridge top. The kettle is in the closet. It'll calm her down."

I'm not sure if the brandy needs to wash out of the woman's system before we can put her back on meds. "She just had tea," I say.

"Oh. She did. Black tea makes her pee."

The man doesn't say anything else, except to ask me if I needed help cleaning up the woman. I've never cleaned a woman before.

I walk the woman to the washroom. It's easy so far. I realize the woman is not resisting me anymore. The boy follows us. "Make sure the water is not too hot," he says before taking over. "Let me show you." I watch him help the woman take off her soiled clothes down to her underwear. Then he tests the water and seats her on a plastic chair under the shower, helps her foam her own body. I notice he has a large, frayed towel around his neck with which he sponges her wet body before helping her put on a fresh set of clothes. Everything looks easy. Ever since the man walked into the apartment, the woman has given up resisting.

The man sits in the kitchen, closely watching, until the woman eats her breakfast, cold, from the casserole, without a word, and then she takes her meds and slides back into her bed. Then the man walks into his dark bedroom and pulls the door behind him, not firmly, but carefully leaving a tiny gap between the door and the frame, as if to indicate he's there, he isn't gone.

With one more hour to kill, I shuffle around the woman's bed as she sleeps. The woman's side of the room is like a three-sided rectangle; the fourth wall is like the dragons' teeth, fitted with an array of narrow storage shelving. Small idols of Hindu gods have been Velcroed on the shelves. I've seen similar idols in our Lorne Park house, stacked inside a box next to the laundry room, waiting to be brought out once a year in the fall. I'm not sure if the gods have been placed in a pecking order. On the top shelf of the closet shrine, a velvet book is streaked with a thick layer of dust. It seems like a book at first—a book that hasn't been opened in a long time—but it's not a book. I want to pull it down from its high perch and check it out. Then I realize the woman is wide awake. She's watching me.

"Do you remember the names of all the gods here?" I ask.

"What's *your* name?" She stares blankly, past my shoulder as if I wasn't there at all, as if the sun behind my back has consumed me in the whole.

"Kal."

"What kind of a name is that?"

The boy chortles again. "He's family, Grandma."

"What religion are you?"

I don't answer.

"Let me see what you're talking about." The woman drags herself to the edge of the bed abruptly. The boy rushes to steady her. She shrugs him off with force. The boy laughs as if he knows his grandma too well. He knows the odds stacked against her. He knows how impossible it would be for the woman to navigate the maze of randomly placed furniture right up to the closet shrine, on the other end of the room, without help. When he reaches out to help again, the woman accepts his hand as if it's the most natural thing, as if they've played that game before.

Now facing her shrine, the woman stands still, observing the idols—made from mud, glass, wood—the silk tassels fluttering on the velvet pad cushions. When she tries removing one, the idols are stuck. She looks at the boy. The boy untangles them off the Velcro and hands them over, one at a time. She grabs an idol, examines it in the flushed light, looks away as if she's trying to recall something about it from a faraway place before returning it to the boy. I stand watching as the woman completes what seems like a ritual of remembrance. The boy snaps the little idols back exactly where he retrieved them from.

"Don't you want to look inside the box?" the boy asks, pulling the box off the top shelf and, in a flash, ripping it out of the velvet casing. Then he holds it out for the woman to see.

The woman fumbles, trying to grab the box. The boy helps her open it. Inside, I see a cluster of gold rings and pearls, dulled with age; earrings and necklaces and a silver choker, black in the hollows, studded with tiny pieces of sapphire around the mesh and a large amethyst dead centre; and right beside it, another hollow made by a set of serrated silver bangles stacked up like a tiny cylinder, and inside it, a plastic ball, blue like her good eye.

"There it is." The woman snatches the ball and slams it into her left eye, through the folds of flesh. The ball doesn't fit flush into the dark cavity. She slams it in again. Then she tries to walk back excitedly, navigating the furniture maze by herself before she trips, and her head hits the edge of the bed. The ball rolls off the socket of her eye.

When the boy rushes to grab it, the woman pushes him away, slumping on the floor on all fours, pushing hard, like an animal in labour, she drags herself down the arc of the plastic ball that has rolled the length of the floor and now stands still against the wall at the far end of the partitioned room, right by the chair where the boy sat earlier.

As he tries again to help her back to her feet, the woman

takes his hand, grabs the fallen eye with both hands, rubs it against the sleeve of her gown, pops it back in, and slowly pulls herself up.

On the table, when she notices the hand-drawn dragons—all four of them stacked on top of each other—she touches them, then she brings them closer to her good eye, examines them closely. She seems to know something about the four dragons that makes her look at the boy instantly. The boy chortles. Then the woman pulls the chair, seats herself, and looks at the dragons again. Now the boy laughs, embarrassed at his own work. She laughs back, and they're both laughing and, in that moment, as her hair falls over and clouds her face, she pulls it back in a reflex and coils it up at the back, exactly as in the picture of her in the rain.

"What's the matter?" The man appears briefly at the door, stares at the drawings, and returns to his room. Aunt Rita stays seated on the chair, now grinning as if she knows the story the boy has secretly coded into the drawings and is unable to hold back her joy in unlocking it.

When the clock strikes four, it is already past my time to leave. The man is back in his room, apparently asleep; the sound of his snoring comes on and off between the grind of the AC. I know I don't have to wait. I change out of my scrubs, collect my things. The boy walks me to the door and hands me the dragons. Then he tries to grab the package and drag it inside. The package is much bigger than his arms. I stop him. "Let me do it," I say.

"Will I see you tomorrow?" He stares at me hopefully, as if he cares that his words come through as a wish rather than a question.

"Maybe," I say. At that point, I truly don't know.

2015

BRAMPTON

~NILOY

Hands Like Trees

The woman who bought the *Bristlecone on Rock* insisted she wanted the canvas mounted rather than rolled in a tube. When I met her in the garage, she reminded me of Jörg. She had the same cleft lip and gun-metal eyes. But she had no hair, and her skin hung loosely around her arms and neck as if she had suddenly lost a lot of weight. She used a stick, walked very slowly, and her face was so blanched, it seemed she was fighting a disease.

After she left, I looked at the roughs again and thought about what she had said—what had made her drive the eighty kilometres from Oshawa chasing the piece *like an obsession—how each branch looked like her own gnarled hand touching a piece of the sky*. I hadn't thought of it before—hands . . . like trees. But it reminded me of something else: when I was in grade school, I was obsessed with drawing hands. It was also when I first met Jörg.

About three months after my parents separated, Mom invited Jörg for dinner. He lived two streets down the crescent. Mom had known him for a long time as they worked in the same nursing school where Jörg was a pharmacy consultant. He was about forty at that time—ten years back—with a shock of naturally curly golden hair. He was five foot seven or eight with extra-broad shoulders and looked evenly proportioned on all sides, like a square, except for his paunch. Mom had ordered in from the corner curry shop. I remember there was a problem with the food. The cumin rice was greasy, the tamarind slurry of the goat vindaloo much less hot than Jörg had had on his trip to India. He insisted on cooking it himself the next time he was invited.

During dinner, I watched Jörg. He had really large hands. Large and hairy and pink. Even though he talked about food—why palm vinegar is way better than white—the way he moved his hands to reveal a freshly minted loonie before making it disappear made me feel special. I made him do it twice. He said he'd teach me. He waved his hands, grasping imagined objects, asking me to guess what was inside. If I guessed right, he opened his hand and let it go. It was a game. I was thirteen. I liked him instantly.

The following Saturday, Jörg returned to deliver on his promise of vindaloo and cumin rice. Since Mom had separated, we had moved into an apartment in a boxy building in Bramalea closer to her work. Jörg took over the kitchen. It was tiny, but he moved like a magician.

The Saturday after that, we went to Fletcher's Creek, and Jörg helped me capture a tree frog in a pickle jar for my grade-school project. It was a year after Grandma went to the retirement home. A week later, Mom heard from Calcutta. My grandpa, who would be ninety in a year, had suffered another fall. Mom worried this might be a sign of worse things to come. I couldn't entirely follow their conversation in Bengali, but I knew Grandpa had been through this earlier. The first time he slipped and fell in the bath, Mom was on the phone with a local doctor for hours. I think she felt responsible for anything bad that happened to Grandpa in India, since she was the one who had brought Grandma here. I could tell matters were far more serious this time when Mom announced we'd be travelling to Calcutta to bring Grandpa over to live with us.

"Where?" I didn't know Grandpa at all, except in photos with a military hat.

"What do you mean 'where'? In our guest room."

"What about Grandma? Will you bring her back home?"

"You mean will they forget everything and restart? I'm not sure."

I didn't want to go to Calcutta because the last time I visited, I was sick the entire time. But when Jörg said he'd come along, I knew I was going.

He knew a lot of tricks. Like he could rotate his fingers in opposite directions without moving the wrist, and he could remove his thumb off his hand or make his hands pass through each other. We hung out a lot. I felt I understood him better than my mother because she was always trying to figure him out. I wanted him to move in with us. But Mom, who was generally encouraging of the bonding time between us, didn't seem to want that. Not right away. "That's not how we do things," she said as if she needed more time to decide. I thought Mom was being a prude, because I had seen them kissing.

Jörg claimed this would be his second visit to India. He said he had trekked the Himalayas for a month, right after his graduation. He said he knew exactly what shots we needed to take beforehand, all the ointments, lotions, and meds we needed to carry in June, during the start of the monsoon season, none of which Mom had ever taken notice of in our earlier travels. I knew Jörg was right. I was sick on my earlier visits. I wouldn't go without them.

In Calcutta, Mom stayed out all day visiting aunts and uncles but rarely with Jörg. I overheard her say that she wasn't yet comfortable being seen with him among relatives who had yet to know that she and Dad had separated. Given no choice, Jörg grudgingly stayed back in the mornings, moseying around the sprawling property with a pair of rusty hedge clippers, trimming the bougainvillea and cacti in the terrace garden or tending the tomatoes. Or he'd visit the kitchen, trying to talk to the Bengali cook using gestures and signs he claimed epicures intuitively understood the world over. Right after five, as the first shadows showed up on the grilled second-floor verandah of the ancient three-storey, colonial-style house, Jörg stepped out alone with a camera around his shoulder. I wanted to go out with him, but Grandpa wouldn't let me.

"Be careful," he warned Jörg the first time he heard he'd left the house alone.

"Careful of what?" Jörg knew what he was doing.

But Grandpa behaved like he had to tutor Jörg whenever he had the chance. "This city can surprise you. You can't master it off the internet."

Jörg said he knew more about Calcutta than Mom, which was true because Grandpa said, "That's hardly promising because Toshie knows nothing." And he laughed.

Jörg laid it on thick whenever he had a chance. I didn't mind. Mom doubted him. We had argued about that. I thought it took a special kind of courage to stick one's neck out and hype things up. Mom said that's not courage. It's hubris. I didn't know what it meant. But she hated it. My dad hyped everything down. She thought he was passive. She hated that, too. Nobody I knew was a "positivist" like Jörg said he was. It was a new word.

"What kind of photographs can put a positive spin on a dead city?" Grandpa had this nagging curiosity about Jörg that almost bordered on suspicion. He had never seen a white person up close before. The way he poked and prodded Jörg, it was borderline harassment.

"I guess it's the history," Jörg tried to explain. He was good at explaining.

"But what's there outside? There's nothing left—all gone. Take photos of this house instead. Do you know how much history sits on these walls?"

Jörg said it was the people that he was crazy about—the cotton fluffers, knife sharpeners, key makers, houseware vendors, and the street kids who seemed to follow him everywhere.

"Like flies?" Grandpa was always testing.

"Like fish—their black eyes—either flashing in the sun or dead still and dreaming." He spoke quietly, unlike everyone else in Calcutta, who spoke loudly in a higher pitch, often saying the same thing over and over as if they needed to repeat everything three times before anyone would believe what they said.

"Make sure you watch your wallet." Grandpa didn't get Jörg.

Jörg said he was also scouting street food recipes. Bazaars, bistros, canteens, coffee houses, street kitchens, he was doing it all. Grandpa scoffed when Jörg wasn't watching. But I believed him. I could totally picture Jörg in the bazaar. I liked it when he was around since he made everything "magical" and pulled Mom away from all the stress she had to deal with lately. I missed Jörg the moment he left the house. I wanted to be with him always. But the humidity outside made me sick. That and the crowded streets where everyone brushed against everyone all the time. I hated strangers touching me. When Jörg was gone, I felt like translating and defending and channelling him because of Grandpa's strange, annoying questions.

"You mean people back there are interested in things we eat, not just in Buddha statues?" Grandpa asked over a game of chess.

"No one eats the stuff you make us eat."

The first few days, Jörg and Mom synched their return precisely so we could all sit down for dinner together. A team of part-time house-helps trooped in daily to assist with the chores. Grandpa ran the affairs as the grand old patriarch. Watching him holler directions to his army of helpers, it was hard to imagine he'd feel comfortable anywhere else. I knew Mom was wasting her time. But for Grandpa's constant shortness of breath and forever racing heart, it was hard to tell he was recovering from a dislocated hip. He had the house-helps clean every corner and cook all kinds of Bengali meals almost every day; sometimes he'd have the same chore done twice over if he hadn't seen it done with his own eyes the first time, or if he forgot seeing it done. I thought, perhaps, even Mom knew Grandpa wasn't ready yet to travel thousands of miles just to be dumped into an elder care with Grandma. Then, all of a sudden, he suffered a stroke in his sleep and died the same night.

I stopped eating, didn't get out of my room. It was so abrupt; I couldn't believe it.

After the thirteen days of mourning, when it was time to leave, I contracted severe stomach flu and Mom extended our stay so she could sell the house and close out. Jörg took over the cooking. Never in his life had Jörg cooked on a gas burner with cast iron pots and kitchen implements, but he was a natural. And he had this uncanny ability to persuade people to do things that were hard, like changing the cooking method from pan frying to stir-frying and the cooking fat from mustard oil to coconut oil. He downloaded recipes at the local internet café, researched ingredients, visited farmers' markets, haggled prices, and took copious notes he claimed would surely become the cookbook that would launch a hundred Bengali restaurants back in Canada. No one took him seriously. But it was fun just to dream about it.

After a while, Mom became possessive of Jörg in a weird way. The way he claimed anything exotic or strange that came his way—made it his own and then moved on—made her insecure. She worried Jörg would get bored with us and move on. She wanted to keep him, but she didn't know how. Mom had suddenly aged or tired or maybe given up. She spent all day closeted in Grandpa's room doing nothing—shuffling old photographs like a deck of cards, giving away clothes, silverware, and a vast array of knick-knackery that hung on every wall like a museum, while Jörg took control of the house and the entourage of house-helps who were steadily being let go.

When Mom wasn't in Grandpa's room, she was entertaining relatives who were still streaming in from distant places to offer condolences, or she was giving a house tour to the long lineup of property developers keen to relieve her of the unwanted landlady role she had been thrust into. Jörg made sure to announce the carte du jour right at breakfast. "Start with the end," he'd wink and lay down the dessert options first because he knew I had a sugar fetish. I don't remember ever getting as much attention from anyone. I was impatient for the trip to end, to get back home. I knew Mom had reached the point where she couldn't do without Jörg. I knew she needed him, but she was also scared. He was unreal.

All morning, Jörg would sing to himself, gathering, preparing, cooking, and tasting. After he was done cooking, he raised the pitch of his burnished baritone and had the kitchen cleaned, making sure no traces were left behind on any of the implements he had used, as that was one thing he hated—"evidence of the hunt." Afternoons, I stayed quarantined in my little room upstairs, busy with my iTunes, occasionally chatting with friends on Jörg's phone. But I never mentioned Jörg to anyone, scared to share even a tiny bit of the experience of watching him, a strange magic giant inside this strange museum-house, thousands of miles away. He said I needed to keep it a secret.

At lunch, Jörg would be the lone person talking, trying hard to explain what he had found out earlier that morning about asafoetida—how it came to be known as God's food and devil's dung—and nigella and cumin, and fenugreek and fennel—the magic ingredients missing in his recipes. Mom would absent-mindedly work her food—usually curried fish and rice—occasionally raising her head, appearing attentive, sometimes letting out gasps of approval at something Jörg said or did, but I knew it was all fake. Mom was tiring out from trying to measure up. Mom tired of everything too soon. But it was different for me. It was as if a new chapter in my life was opening up. Even as I felt tired and was literally pulled down by the afternoon sting of the flu that always seemed to follow the carrot-sweet and black-pepper Bengali chicken soup, I'd be back to bed ready for more Jörg time.

He'd attend to me like a personal butler, making sure I took the prescriptions that he had figured out. He'd make a show, bringing the coloured capsules on a dry white saucer with a glass of water half-filled, "just so nothing spills over." He'd wait as I washed the meds down in one impatient gulp, then he'd hang around, quietly cancelling out the noise outside—incessant street calls hawking all sorts of things—shutting doors and windows, drawing the curtains, weaning me off the headphones. At that point, I liked to wait for directions, do exactly as told. Like an apprentice at the magic show.

"Sea diet and siesta, that's what the world needs." He'd start again, seating himself on a corner of the bed, talking about all the things we'd do once we were back: the spices, the socks, the salt lamp, the incense burners, and the batik yoga cushions he had to get for all the folks back home who impatiently awaited our return, folks I didn't know, and I'd want to know them all. He'd talk about the chalk-white teeth of street kids he had photographed. About the farmers in the market, how their faces lit up when they saw him, and how their shoulders drooped when they found out he could out-haggle them at their own game. I knew the antibiotics would put me to sleep soon, but I wanted him to carry on, hoping I could stay awake a little longer, battle my eyes as they became heavy, battle my mind as it shut down, and Jörg, like a magician, went on.

"How many different types of street vendor calls can you imitate?"

By the time Jörg reached this point, I'd see the shapes of words oozing out from his red, cleft, bee-stung lips. Words—conjoined like a train of coloured soap bubbles—floating under the beams of the high ceiling, a chameleon's tongue moving from the dark cavern inside his mouth towards my body, penetrating the sheets, touching me everywhere or just sitting there—distinct and languid and effortless, defying gravity—gliding, stirring, quickening the heartbeat; and the sounds from his throbbing mouth would mix with sounds from the radio seeping in from Grandpa's room, where Mom took her afternoon nap. Soon Jörg would be gone, I knew. I wanted him to stay. Beyond that, I can't remember a thing.

When I woke up, it'd be Mom by the edge of the bed, freshly showered, dressed casually, ready for the evening. But I'd be aching.

"Is it fever or something else?" Mom couldn't handle all that sickness. "How long ago did you sit on the throne? Have you ever had to wait this long? Should we see a doctor? Where did Jörg disappear to again?"

She'd tire me out with all those questions. I could hardly bear to see her. But I felt it, a dreadful ache in the butt. Aching in a way I had never known before. This wasn't just the regular stiffness. Drained, restless, and sore, I'd hear the helps, the last ones who had evaded the mass firing, trying to cheer me up. I'd remember, to my relief, Jörg returning, quickly taking charge, retrieving from his pouch a pain-killer I so desperately needed.

Later, as the night progressed, almost as in a dream, I'd walk downstairs to see folks dressed in sarees and sherwanis like ancient courtiers coming through the doors, parading about before banding around the ancient teak table, chatting about time past, Grandpa and Grandma. I'd hear them talk about the food Jörg had spent the entire day preparing. I'd hear the loud ooh-oohs as Jörg carefully served each course in the proper order.

A few months after we returned from Calcutta, the school wanted to talk to Mom. *No one's home*, I had lied earlier. So they sent a letter. For an entire evening, I saw it on the console table, the school emblem on the white cover, standing out among the flyers and other peanut-coloured envelopes carrying bills. I knew what the letter was about. I wanted to destroy it without anyone noticing, but Mom got to it. She called Dad. She had no choice.

I wasn't nervous, just numb, when I heard my parents had been summoned to school. I remember, the meeting at the principal's office lasted the entire forty-five minutes of science class. Halfway through the meeting, I noticed the vice-principal walking in to fetch my homeroom teacher, who took away the box that contained all the binders with my drawings. It would be a shock to them. I knew.

I knew that because Dad didn't live with us anymore,

he'd blame everything on Mom. For weeks, I'd been having a hard time even being seated at any one place in school. No one cared. I'd see something, a switch would get flipped setting off a reaction, shutting me down completely. I'd start shivering, pimples would break out all over my skin, my heartbeats would quicken. It was like something had invaded my body and got me all worked up. A hand hammering away at my chest. Breathless, I moved around just to get the hand off my body; get the hand off the hammering and nailing and clawing; get the hand away from a black box, empty and waiting. I moved from the class to the café, from the café to the library, from the library to the gym, all the while searching for an exit door, out of the gym, out of the school, out of my body. Soon I was in the parking lot, watching cars pass by the street out front. No longer in control of my body, with no sense of time, no real memory of how I got there, no idea what I'd do next. Not until someone got me back.

Usually, it was the vice-principal. In class, I'd follow along for a bit, then fall off the grid again, staring blankly at the open page of the book on the table. The print on the page converged into a black mass—the shape of an animal, or an animal tongue, the shape of an animal hand—hairy and fluid like a snake in the grass, and I knew it was just a dream. I'd hear whispers: *I won't tell anyone. I know it's a secret. I know how to keep a secret.* I couldn't shake it off. So I started drawing them out just to stop thinking about those hands—in different positions, doing different things—

clawing, digging, scraping, touching. Caught up in the act of drawing hands, I'd become free. No longer suffocated. No longer breathless.

When the meeting ended, I remember feeling light in my head, almost weightless. I had to hold on to my seat. I knew my secret was no longer a secret. I felt I had floated up and my eyes were frozen looking out the window, out at this new world, as leaves from a maple in the schoolyard fell in a yellow bleed leaving the branches with nothing.

"Why are you doing *this*?" Mom, as usual, couldn't hide the disappointment in her voice.

I wish I knew. I remember looking out of the car just to get the strength to say something that could make it all go away. I remember Mom fighting for air as she drove through the rain, as the dampness in the red corners of her eyes exploded and rolled down, melting her face instantly. But I also knew she wouldn't let me fail.

No one said a word, not even Dad, who usually had *something* to say in such situations. Back in our little apartment, I shot back to my room and locked myself in. After some time, when Dad picked the lock and peeked inside, I looked at him from inside the darkness that stood solid like a wall between us. Somehow it felt like he was the one responsible for every bad thing happening to us.

Dad looked at me strangely, the edge of his face softened in the light flooding in from the hallway. His shrunken frame, his gutted face, the sheer failure about him threw me off. I remember that. I never hated him when he and Mom fought, but I hated him right then. I clipped the headphones back on, stone-still, as Dad flipped the light switch on, and off, before making room for himself on the edge of the bed.

"What song is playing?" he asked after a while. I hated his voice, the hollowness of it. I couldn't meet his eyes again. I wanted the wall to stay in place forever. Then I cranked up the volume so I didn't have to hear him at all. I knew the music was leaking out of my headphones. I knew he couldn't tell which track was playing. He didn't know me at all. I wanted him gone.

Of all the recommended therapists, Dr. Popov was closest to home. Mom just had one need, that the therapist be a complete stranger so that no one in the community would know I was seeing one. He had grey eyes and wore thick-rimmed glasses. He had an efficient manner about him and a steady stock of clever non sequiturs he delivered with deadpan seriousness. He was easy. He let me draw as long as I wanted. But it wasn't until the third or the fourth session that I could respond to his questions with anything other than monosyllables. I wanted to get better, but I didn't think he could really help me. After the sixth or the seventh session, he could get me to relax and fall asleep; by the tenth, I remember visiting his office and not feeling like I needed to draw hands anymore. He could get me into a trance when he wanted. After the sessions, I'd only remember the questions I couldn't answer—

"Is it one voice or many?"

"What's in the hand?"

"Where are you now?"

"Who's inside the black box?"

During the graduation-day ceremony at school, Mom seemed grateful that they let me graduate middle school at all. I had missed all last term. In the first year of high school, several things happened in such close succession, I had a hard time separating one from the other. I found I liked drawing other things. Trees. The new obsession. Later I found N., an art major several years senior, and I had my first taste of weed in the back of an old Ford, his father's. Then we started driving to faraway places looking for trees in the oddest possible shapes—gnarled, twisted, knotted—the freakier the better.

"Where's Jörg?" I did ask.

Mom said he was gone. I didn't disbelieve her. I knew Mom was worried he'd be gone. I knew Mom couldn't keep anyone too long.

"Gone where?"

"He called once and then he was gone."

"You never looked for him?"

"For what?" Mom didn't want to talk about Jörg.

I told Mom what that woman buyer of my *Bristlecone* had to say about the piece. Mom said she knew I was drawing the same tree over and over.

"Where's Jörg now?"

"What?"

"Do you have a photograph?"

"Stop doing that. Enough trees."

The same night, I dreamt I was in middle school. The windows in our homeroom are wide open. A cloud has burst into class. Everything is covered in fog. Dense fog. I'm trying hard to find the sketch I just made—the maple outside the window that had been bleeding yellow in the schoolyard is gone.

I knew Mom had saved all my hand drawings from middle school inside a portfolio under her bed. I had seen them earlier. But I was scared to look again. In the ten years since I last looked at them. Scared of the strange power they seemed to have. I can't remember how often I had this dream where the hands sprang out of the metal spine of the binder and reached for me—magically—just the hands, severed from the body. It has been a while since that dream came back. I'm less scared now.

As I pulled at the portfolio, a yellow legal envelope slid out from underneath the case. I knew what that was. It had my name printed on it and a sticker on the top left with Dr. Popov's name and address. The word *Confidential* stamped on it in red ink still bright, undiminished. I could sense a shiver as I held the report. It was raining outside. A window was open. I was uncertain what would happen just from touching it.

Past the cover page that showed the date, I flipped through the rest, stopping briefly at the transcripts of every interview I had had. In the section with my family history, I couldn't fail to notice again that Dad had already fought cancer back when we left our old house and moved into the apartment. I flipped through the achievement tests I remembered taking, the long list of diagnosed disorders, summary observations: *Tactile Hallucinations—likely cause for anxiety, depression, somatization.* I still have no clue what any of it means.

As I returned the envelope to the drawer, I realized Mom had come upstairs looking for me. I flipped the portfolio open and laid the hand drawings down on her bed just to see if they still meant anything. Surely, the woman was right; the fingers looked like branches of the *Bristlecone* I just sold. Who was that woman? Could that be Jörg, dressed in drag, checking out?

I could sense Mom walking into the room, standing beside me, watching. We didn't say anything for a long time, but I did notice she was fighting to breathe. Panting, as if she, too, had been in the spell of those hands and didn't want them out in the open. But why then didn't she get rid of them? Perhaps she was waiting for a day when something would happen, someone would come, make everything all right, and I'd find the strength to toss them out.

I didn't want to toss them out. If the hands are in the trees, I want to keep them. I don't want to stop doing trees.

Mom searched my face as I moved away from her. It was September. A cloud had burst into the room through the open window. It seemed she was trying to find me in the fog as I stowed the drawings back in the portfolio. We never talked about those hands again. We rarely talked about the trees. We didn't have to.

2017

TORONTO

JOY

Something Happened

I was in my senior year of college. It was about the end of August. My summer term had long ended, but I was still hanging around campus. All my friends were gone. Home. Or on backpacking trips around the world. I didn't want to be home. Mom had moved out. I hadn't been talking to Dad. Then I heard Gina had moved into our Parklawn house with Clara. It was like a stab in the back.

I knew he was dating Gina, his long-time associate at the law firm he had founded with his friends from U of T. I had met Gina a few times at his office parties. Always in stilettos or pumps, she was about five foot ten. She had deep brown eyes and dark hair that she had a hard time keeping in check. Her husband had a walking disorder, I think, as I always saw him with a stick and an odd bucket hat as if he didn't want anyone to realize how much shorter than Gina he was. Gina's daughter, Clara, had gap teeth and metal braces, spoke with a lisp, and was some sort of dance prodigy. She'd never turn down a chance to perform at Dad's office parties, doing her pieces, like a professional, with a flourish, as if she had rehearsed them a thousand times. I never thought it would come to this.

Soon I'd be gone, too. For a year-long internship with Oxfam in Abuja, Nigeria. And that would be the end. Because even though I was adopted when I was five years old, this was the only real family I had ever had.

Then Dad called. He said he had an important announcement to make. He wanted me to come up home for Thanksgiving, which was weeks away, right around the time when I'd be leaving. He paused when I said that, as if to gather strength, before he could put on his lawyer suit and launch into an argument, which he often did, even for matters he didn't care about. I waited for his typical list of threes—compelling reasons for me to be home for Thanksgiving before I was gone. When that didn't happen, I sensed something had changed there, too. The usual presumption was missing in his voice. I sensed a hesitation, even distance, as if he were asking for a favour. The general elections were around the corner and some of my class friends from pol-sci had signed up for campaigns closer to home. I said yes.

I spent the first few days of the Thanksgiving week at Mom's new house in Burlington, a few blocks from her work. She was still busy with late-summer showings. Yet we were able to go out fishing Thursday afternoon, down at Grindstone Creek. It was strange watching her in short, dyed-blond hair, long leather boots, and a fishing jacket, enjoying herself in the sun. I had never seen her so free and happy before, rigging the pole with Trilene, stringing the bobber, baiting the hook with salted minnows.

She was with a friend who was patient and skillful and careful in the way she held on to Mom's waist, steadying her as she shivered in the chill or cast the line eagerly, like a young apprentice waiting for the tug. Something had caught the hook. It turned out to be a wild brook trout the size of her hand. They took a selfie—mouths open, tongues sticking out, the catch hanging between their faces pressing into each other; then they let it out into the wild. I realized their relationship was now official. But Mom asked me not to read too much into what I saw at the creek. I was still her bestie. She had a room for me in her new apartment.

The same evening, I took the GO train home. Dad picked me up at Long Branch station. He was still in his gym clothes. I could smell his sweat. When I was younger, and he'd be gone for weeks to Detroit or Chicago or Pittsburgh, attending clients, I often lay down beside Mom and pressed his pillow on my face, just for the smell of him. I noticed he had started growing a medium-sized beard, trimmed sharp; the deep brown tint on his hair looked strange against the sun.

We stopped, first at an Italian bakery, where he chatted up the bald, sweaty owner about the soccer unfolding on the small, old-time TV, before picking up slabs of preordered Gorgonzola and Taleggio and pecorino Toscano. Then we were at the LCBO, where he grabbed craft beer and Bacardi, and finally at the pet store.

Dad said he had always wanted a dog, but Mom wouldn't let him. Mom was allergic to dog saliva. "But now Gina's dog has moved in. And I'm able to see the dog's point of view. The way they look at you, you feel their soul is on their tongue. It's entirely possible I was a dog in my previous life." He didn't move his eyes off me until I smiled.

Dante was a three-year-old golden retriever. Dad showed me several pictures on his phone. One that stayed with me had Dante squatting in the middle of a sidewalk and Dad prostrated on the green strip next to the curb, looking into his eyes. He said Dante and he had become friends to a point where he didn't mind when the dog occasionally crawled into the bed "like a child who is so needy for love, you feel you'd stop everything else and just be Dad." Same thing again. He stared until I showed some sort of appreciation. He was trying hard to break the ice.

By the time we reached home, the yard door was open invitingly. Gina was in a floral green summer dress, her dark hair skittering in the breeze as she worked fresh cobs and lamb chops on the grill. It was getting dark. Clara, who had been out somewhere, walked through the yard door in her joggers and a black open-back top, her pink skin freckled with red and brown spots like a hawk fish. We sat and ate in the backyard to the sound of cicadas. After a couple of beers, Dad started talking about the dinner they had planned for Sunday. Gina's parents were early diners, so the party would start around six. Gina's three sisters and their families would come in early as they were all scattered around the GTA—Woodbridge and Vaughan—and her brother lived in Georgetown. There would be confetti and fireworks: blue or pink—they were going to keep it a secret until the gender reveal "for the newbie," Dad said as Gina blushed.

So this was the big announcement. I felt Clara was staring at me before she started coughing as if something had stuck in her throat. Then she stopped, smiled at me, and quickly looked away. She was in her senior year at high school, and with her thick black hair bunned at the top of her head and bushy eyebrows arched above the bridge of her nose, she looked much older than seventeen. She was prepping for the big leap into pre-professional ballet. "Training eighty hours each week," Dad said jokingly. Or proudly. It was hard to tell.

"Do you give performances?" I asked.

"Yes," she looked at me squarely, without hesitation. "There's one next week if you'd like to stay."

"How long are they?"

"Hour and half."

But before I could reply, Dad continued to lay down the details of the dinner as they had planned: "a grand fusion of two ancient cuisines." There would be two turkeys—"one stuffed with curried goat and the other pure vegan." At which point Gina and Clara burst out laughing. He said it smoothly and with a straight face; I couldn't tell if he had rehearsed the gaffe ahead of time.

For desserts, there would be two kinds of pies. "No

pumpkin." Because even though he liked it, no one in Gina's family could stand the flavour. So it would have to be rice pudding on almond crust and rum-soaked raisins for one and double-crust apple for the other—Clara's favourite. "And for you," he added, pointing his crisply trimmed face towards me, "a special order of the cinnamon ricotta squares from your favourite bakery in Lorne Park." I had grown up eating those. He liked those more than me.

After we were done with the beers, Gina said she had to step out to walk Dante, and on her way back, she'd get some dessert for the night and also a few spices she was still missing for the curried goat recipe. The metro was a few blocks away and it had gotten dark. Dad said he'd come along and help her pick the spices, only if Gina could give him a few minutes. It was beginning to get chilly. Gina and Clara went inside.

Dad said, "Come on." I wasn't sure what he meant before I figured he wanted to give me a little tour of the house—walk me through the changes they had made "since the time you permanently moved out." This he said with a wink, darting a quick glance to make sure I understood it was my fault if I found any of the changes too radical or disagreeable.

He showed me the new paintings on the living room walls—oil-on-canvas reproductions of Botticelli's *Venus* replacing the gold-framed still life with quince and apples and pears Mom had got at a yard sale several years back, and *The Kiss* by Francesco Hayez replacing the Sears family portrait from the time Mom still visited the Mata G. spiritual centre in Brampton and, on special occasions, used the red cosmetic powder along the part in her long black hair. I was so small in the portrait, I could be neatly folded in her lap. On the wall facing the kitchen, a portrait of Mata G.—an evangelist Mom's family believed in—was gone, as was the astral blue handmade kantha quilt—the only remaining bequest from my grandmother—that Mom had cut into strips like a collage covering the entire wall. There were pot lights everywhere, replacing the crystal chandeliers Mom had brought from her family's home in India; the hand-painted terracotta vases Mom made at a pottery workshop, gone, too—replaced with nothing in particular, just empty spaces. Suddenly, the living room that had always appeared claustrophobic had become roomy. The stained-glass dining table had been replaced by a large wood table and the backs of the wrought-iron chairs were now covered with ivory sleeves.

As I started upstairs, Dad began walking the opposite way, down to the basement.

"Come on down," he said.

"Why?"

"I found a place with the best imported grapes. I got a crusher. I'm brewing my own wine—Muscat and Alicante. And now, look here, our little cheese cave."

"What kinds?" I said out of curiosity, but my throat felt dry, as if I was talking against my will, to a stranger.

"Italian blue and farm cheddar."

I took a peek inside the stand-up freezer. The three slabs of cheese on the top shelf sat neatly on bamboo mats. I could see mould growing on them unevenly; it smelled like damp dirt. "Are they ready yet?"

"Almost. The problem with the stand-up freezer is that water keeps dripping between the shelves, and you can't really control the moulding, or we'd be done. But we can open one of those tomorrow and see."

My bookcase and chest of drawers had been brought down and stacked around the walls of the room Mom often used for her friends from the Mata G. Centre when they came visiting. My old bed was made up and waiting for me. A few boxes with Mom's stuff—mainly portraits of Mata G. that she had never put up on the wall after we moved from Brampton to this larger house—were stashed in the little mud room with the walkout under the deck. Suddenly I felt suffocated and went for the patio doors to get some air, but Dad pulled me towards the cellar to show me the wines he had collected—mostly Italian—the names of which I no longer remember. He had a map of Italy tacked to the wood door, with its twenty wine regions, colour-coded to match the handwritten stickers on the frame of the wood cellar shelves he had custom made.

I had known Dad to be a scotch fanatic, so this passion for brewing and collecting wines was all new to me, and fascinating, but I knew it was also his nature to dive headfirst into anything new. He started telling me about the late-summer vacation they were planning the following year that would include a tour of all the Italian wine regions highlighted on the map "to put a place to the taste." He said they'd rent a cottage in Tuscany—Gina and her whole family—to watch the wine-making festivals in Chianti and Chiusi and Sant'Antonio, and then travel south to hunt down a decent one-dollar home in Zungoli. He asked if I'd like to come along.

"I might have a job by then." I knew he wasn't serious.

He laughed and said he was hoping to get handyman lessons from Gina's brother, a building contractor who would be officially appointed in charge of the Sicilian reconstruction when he got here for the party. He stared and waited until I laughed. Until the sounds of the floorboards creaking upstairs and Gina's footsteps on the stairway to the basement got closer, followed by her long shadow. She was checking in to see if Dad still wanted to get out with Dante.

Neither of us had realized we had been down in the basement for almost a half-hour. As Dad hurried back upstairs, Gina asked if I'd like to help out with the party prep.

"I've no real kitchen skills." I hesitated, but when I saw Clara was in the kitchen peeling potatoes, I joined in. After some time, I saw Clara pointing at a gaze of raccoons rummaging through the trash outside. I had put my earbuds back in when I realized that Clara had said something. I stared at her. "What did you say?"

"Why? Haven't you smoked before?" Her bushy eyebrows arched upward.

Of course I had, but Gina and Dad would be back sooner or later. I was afraid the smell would linger a long time in the kitchen or travel around the house, and it could be embarrassing if they snuck up on us from the backyard.

Clara suggested we go up to her room. It felt weird at first, but since Dad had stopped me from going upstairs, I had become curious about all the changes they might have put in place. I walked around the upstairs hallway, slyly opening and closing doors to my bedroom and Mom's, peeking into the interiors I could no longer recognize in the dark. It felt as though I was in a stranger's house—an interested buyer, poking in to assess the lives of the people who now lived in these boxed spaces—and Clara, trailing behind, didn't say a word.

Clara, it seemed, wasn't a habitual smoker. She had a stash inside a chewing-gum container taped to the bottom of the clothes chest. She blocked the bottom of the door with towels, wrapped a plastic air net to the vents, turned off the lights, lit a scented candle, and slid the window upward just a teeny bit to let in some air. All of that so smoothly, it felt like her carefully rehearsed dance movements.

Her hands shook as she rolled the joint, her large hazel eyes looking at me hopefully as she ran the sticky side of the rolling paper between her lips. I could tell from the dank smell, and the difficulty she had lighting the weed, it must have lain in the chest for a while.

Soon we were laughing. We both had earbuds on. I asked

her what she was listening to, and she let me use one of her earbuds. It was Justin Bieber's "Love Yourself." Then she took out her phone and showed me a recital from her most recent performance, then another, then one more. Then she slid her hand around my waist and pulled me towards her. I realized she was getting high, and I could have stopped her right there, but I loosened my body and slid into hers and soon we were kissing. Facing me, fully clothed, she shifted me around so she could spread wide open and jump onto my thighs, wrapping her legs around my waist in the manner of Yoko Ono and John Lennon in the Leibovitz poster stuck to my dad's old closet she now used.

We still had our earbuds criss-crossed into each other's ear, facing the door, and she had started rocking to the beats of Adele's "Hello" when I heard the door behind me shake. At first, I thought it was her legs flapping against the door. Then the door cracked open a tiny bit, and she looked up with effort, her droopy eyelids battling the sudden burst of light from the hallway that now flooded the room. A dark shadow towered over us even as she kept grooving into me, unruffled. Next, I heard a loud shout and sensed Gina's hands digging into my shoulder with such ferocity, I felt she wanted to tear it away. She pulled me down to the floor with Clara still clinging on. Clara seemed to have passed out.

I remember dragging myself out of the room. My head was hurting so badly I wanted to cut it off. I could barely keep it straight as I ran down to the basement and shut the door. I heard Gina yelling after me. I jumped into my bed, pushed the pillow on my face, and when that didn't drown out the sounds, I put my earbuds in, cranked up the music. Beyond that, I don't remember. I might have slept for an hour or two. When I got back up, I felt hungry.

I found a slab of cheddar in the freezer and took a bite; it tasted awful. I thought of the wine, but there were no openers. Upstairs, Dad and Gina were still yelling at each other. I heard the clank of things violently crashing to the floor. Hours later, I could see through the basement window a car pulling up into our driveway and then someone limping out. It wasn't the cops, as I had feared. From the walking stick and the bucket hat, I guessed it was Clara's dad. Gina had stepped out of the house, too, wrapping her arms around her loose housecoat, her hair skittering everywhere like snakeheads in the dark as she approached him; perhaps she wanted to explain. I saw the man raise himself, pull his face really close to Gina's and say something so loud she had to cover her ears, even as Clara quietly slid into the passenger seat. Then they sped off in a rush, crushing the blue pine shrub that stood on the edge of the driveway.

Later, as the front door slammed shut, I heard Dad and Gina yelling at each other again. A taxi pulled up some time later and then Gina was gone, too, Dante with her. I stayed in the basement wondering what to do next, waiting for a chance to explain. What they thought, was not what had happened. But I didn't understand, myself, exactly what had happened. I went to sleep.

It was afternoon the following day when Dad woke me up. He was holding a brown Timmy's bag and a large coffee. He left them on the table by the bed and asked me to shower and come upstairs to help him in the kitchen. Unwilling to face him, I took my time. I was no good in the kitchen anyway. Yet, right from where I was, I could sense the house floating in the smell of food. I thought it must be the stuff from last night—the turkey and the meats, the peeled potato and broccoli—rotting on the kitchen table.

By the time I freshened up and got upstairs, I realized Dad had gone ahead with cooking the meal as he had described earlier, all of it, all by himself. Soon people were walking into our house, people I knew from Dad's work. He couldn't think of anyone else to invite for a Thanksgiving meal at such short notice.

There must have been twenty of them, young lawyers, interns, and clerks. Soon the food was all gone. After that everyone walked out to the patio with their cigarettes and drinks, while one Indian woman, grey and comfortable in her dark formal dress, stayed back in the kitchen and cleaned up.

Later the same night, my father drove me back to school. It rained the whole time. We didn't speak at all. But I observed him occasionally, from the light of the trucks on the 401, tearing through the dark, revealing the sharp edges of his granite face. I could sense something had come over him—rage, regret—I couldn't tell. I kept looking for an opening but had no way past that glassy expression.

When we exited the highway and stopped at the light, I thought I'd break the silence, tell him what had happened between Clara and me, tell him that it was a stupid mistake, that I was sorry we got high, that I let her come on to me when I could have stopped her. I was even ready to tell him how much I resented his new life because he had abandoned Mom, but I knew that wasn't entirely true. I felt sorry for him. He didn't seem to be there at all. It was as if, looking straight ahead at the road, he had escaped his body, a cold empty shell. We were still a few blocks away from my rented apartment. It was just his ghost driving.

"I'm sorry, but nothing happened," I said.

"Don't worry. I know what happened," he said.

"It's not what you think."

"I wasn't born yesterday. I get it."

"No, you don't." Just then the car stopped at a light. I got out of the car. Started walking. He cruised along for a bit. Rolled the window down and seemed to shout something out at me. I wasn't listening. I didn't want it. It was a long walk. I never saw him before I left.

But now when I'm far, I wish I had stopped and explained. Because I heard Clara never came back after that. And I know what he thought had happened was not quite what had happened. We talked, but I could never bring it up with him again.

2019

SANDMAN PARKING LOT

—NILOY

You Don't Know AB

Mom said you had a rough night. They would've put you on antibiotics by now; the pain should ease. Tomorrow we'll know what's wrong, maybe all this blood and sweat is for something better, maybe they'll let you have visitors, we'll see.

Another storm is on its way to pummel the city. You don't know this. I've been driving for XO Limo. It has been over a year. Now waiting outside Sandman in a Porsche Cayenne Premier for Beena K. Tired. Still, I'd take this any day over night security at 301 Bloor. Pays better. Besides, I needed something regular. Beena K. is what you call a regular. She has needed a limo every week for the past six weeks, every day for the past week—some crisis. I think she hit someone. I like Beena K. We're more than regulars. Friends. I think so. Or we were until last night. Last night was bad. It's stuck in my head like a clot. I can't get rid of it. You'd know what I'm talking about.

Something's cooking inside the hotel. I can tell. I've been out in the cold for some time now. I don't know if I'll get any sleep tonight. You could say she's pretty if it wasn't for those grey eyes—they're terrifying. She's about fifty.

Mom said the doctors have been working hard on you. With all this pain, distraction is good for you, she said; it might help the pain. So I started writing this. To clear my mind. It has been over an hour since Beena K. went inside to meet up with this man whose name is Amar or Amal, I don't know for sure. Let's just call him A. He's not my type. After what happened last night, I'm worried about Beena K. spending so much time with him, alone in a hotel room. Worried like she was a lover. I know what you're thinking, and no. There is no sex involved. There can't be. I just want to make it clear. Although she did come close, really close, to asking for it. I think so, anyway. Not once. But every time she asked me to help her off the car seat into her bed, she looked so wasted, I can't blame her for asking me to stay back. It's a different kind of loving with Beena K.—whipped cream and sugar. If you're running on empty, it fills you up real quick and you're no longer empty, but you have a dry mouth.

She looks like some kind of a goddess—Medusa—because of the long braided wig she wears sometimes, and those eyes. She looks at you, and you turn to stone. I didn't know that until last night. Something happened last night.

I said, "Are you alright?" She looked at me and that was it. I turned to stone. And she has a heart face. Even after what happened last night, she called the boss early in the morning and said it has to be me driving her, or she'll go somewhere else. It's that kind of loving. That's why I'm worried. But I don't know how to reach her. She's with A., and I don't know if she's fucking him or if she's in danger. I'll ask for her number tonight, even though that can get me fired. In our company you can't do that—ask clients for their numbers. I'll take the chance. I sure will. At least next time, I'll be able to call when I need to. Like when I'm worried. I'm sure you know what Mom would say. Don't worry. Just do your job. Be the best shoeshine if shining shoes is what you want. I'm just the limo driver. I'm doing my best.

I used to think this gig might go on for a long time. For a year . . . maybe sixteen months—that's how much college I have left. Longer perhaps. Who knows if I'd need this gig after college? Hopefully not. It's just a few hours on weeknights. And all Saturday. Sunday I am off. Works great for me. And everything was perfect until last week, and then this A. washed in. Perhaps it had all been planned.

I write faster in longhand, or it's just because it's Monday. I think it's fear—the dread of being suddenly yanked out of power—a flatline. That's what I worry about. Mom said you're still unconscious. They're getting ready to put you through tests tomorrow. Don't worry, it'll be fine, she says. I don't believe her. They've shut down all visitors—*precautions*, my ass. You might be worse by the time I'm done writing this. Or not. I hope not.

Once you wake up, you'll be surprised how much space they've given you. You wanted space all your life, now you've got it. I know what you'd say: Who needs what you already have? Hopefully, you'll be able to read this, or I could read it to you. When I see you. I don't mind. That is if they let me in. Just me alone. I wouldn't want anyone else, not even Mom. She says I should call back in the morning. I feel so raw right now, I don't want to read this aloud in front of anyone else. I know this will drive Mom mad. Damn that. Mom says look ahead, stay focused. Last night I was looking ahead, staying focused, and tonight I can't because of what Beena K. said before she went into the hotel.

"Don't park near the entrance."

"Why?"

"Someone might see the limo and think I'm in here." Talk of being presumptuous. She likes being invisible. But I need the light. I'll write something quickly and get back into hiding. And I have to keep watching out for Beena K. I don't want her sneaking up behind me suddenly. If I see her, that's it. I'll have to stop. And that will be that for now. She's full-time.

I think I'll see her when she comes out. If she comes out. There aren't many cars in the lot. Mondays are slow. Slower than the weekend. I know that. I was here, not last Saturday, the one before that. They were having some kind of a party at Beena K.'s. She won a grant for her film about someone called Asifa Bano. I don't know Asifa Bano. You'd have known her if you could read. She said her film is based on true events, some kind of a musical documentary. Beena K. says, over there in India, where Asifa Bano is from, if you make films about real people and claim it's true, they get mad. That's why she'll make it here and give her a different name. I don't know about that. Saturday before last, when I was right here, Beena K. had me taxi two of her guests back and forth after the party. Two women in their forties, one with a permanently pursed duck face and the other with a pixie haircut. First, they asked me to drop them at a Keele Street house—a mysterious French-style manor with columns and a hanging balcony. The house had a red Ferrari by the front door, parked all crooked. The porch lights were on, the house lights were on; a shadow against the white sheers on the window by the balcony moved about frantically. Something was going on. The duck-faced woman noticed it as we got closer; she was expecting something bad, and it was right there. "Turn. Turn," she said.

"Where now?"

So I carted them back where we started and something happened there at Beena K.'s, and they wanted to get to a hotel, and I brought them here to the Sandman. I like this hotel, especially the parking. There's always room for the big car. Then they had me stay back.

"How long?"

"It won't be long."

I could have gone, you know, but I stayed. "Don't worry about the billing, just stay." Beena K. wants me to stay every time she has a house party. She likes me doing errands —weed, alcohol, smokes, whatever. That's not my job, but

I don't mind. Mom says it's good to be useful. They usually have their food taken out from this fancy Indian place around the corner. I like the food. They make it taste real spicy, but it's a total rip-off.

The party shift follows the usual arc—I stay in the car for a bit before Faye calls me in on one pretext or another. Faye is Beena K.'s live-in maid. She imported her from Calcutta. I know what you'd say about that. Beena K. was born there, and she and Faye speak the same language as you and Mom even though Faye says she's Anglo-Indian. Faye is about my age. She has a thing for me, I know that. She'd go, Beena ma'am is looking for you. I know she's not. I know Beena K.'s enjoying herself at the party with her girlfriends. But Faye would say something like that just to have me come in.

I like Faye. She got flown over here about the time Beena K. moved in with some big shot realtor who owned a bunch of properties in every town around here before he was dead. Beena K. inherited them all. At the party, they were doing some kind of weed that goes with mangoes. Where would I get mangoes after midnight? Luckily, the Pakistani convenience had it. Faye is naive, you know. Once my hand brushed her, and she gave me the look, as though that alone would make her pregnant; the next moment she wanted to check out the inside of the limo. I'm not making it up. It would have cost me the job if someone saw her in the car with me. We went to her room instead and had root beer. I can't drink when I'm working. She has the entire basement to herself. Lots of space. She made me stay the night; she went, Beena ma'am is throwing up bad, she needs you to stay. Of course. It's all paid for.

At the party, Beena K. had much to drink, smoked some. She's smart. Not me. She needed me to drive her guests, like I said, home or wherever else they wanted to be. The weed they were doing smelled like the blueberry cheesecake Mom used to get for Grandma. All of them in fancy spring coats—so bright and blingy and moonstoned, you'd want to put them on. The last two guests I was talking about—Pixie Hair and Duck Face—had me stay right here at the Sandman until morning. That's when I noticed the empty lot. Hope it won't be that long tonight. I can't be sleeping all day tomorrow. I want to get back to the regular beat. To see you. If they let me. Mom said they might let in visitors tomorrow. I'm tired. It's a tiring job. Last week was horrible. Last night was terrible. By comparison, the week before last was a piece of cake. That's the thing with being a regular: you have a good week, and then everything suddenly turns bad. I was back in my apartment after dropping Pixie Hair and Duck Face. Whipped; in the shower stall washing up; when Beena K. called again. No shit. Just work. She was reminding me about this man A. whom I needed to pick up at the airport. That was last Sunday when A. showed up and screwed up the whole week.

Sunday is when I visit Grandmother at Sunset Village. A day is enough before she forgets me again. But I can't see her every day. Mom does that, right after college, every day, as though it were part of her day. Sundays, I also drop in at Mom's. Yeah, I've moved out. Finally. I like to see how Mom's doing alone without me. So when Beena K. said she needed me on a Sunday, I hated it. She said this man A. was some kind of god from Bollywood with a famous temper.

"Get there on time or you'll have it from him."

A. was flying from Mumbai to premiere his film at some film fest here in TO. He has been at her place for the past week, been the friend with benefits, I suppose, and now he's in this hotel, fucking her. Or dismantling her. After what happened last night, surely that. I think he's finding it hard to return to Beena K.'s mansion just yet. Beena K.'s husband had it custom built. Faye says it's Beena K.'s now—the house, all the properties, and the business—and now she's going to do what she always wanted to: make movies that no one is making.

Faye keeps telling me, Beena K. is long-term, keep her. Faye watches out for me. She's like a sister, but I can't tell her that, or she'd stop calling me inside for root beer.

Soon as A. popped out of the airport gate, I knew it was him. Soon as he got inside the car, he unbuttoned right down to his shirt—hairy chest, oversized gold chain, cologne that smelled like leather. "Why didn't you have a pickup sign for me," he asked. I said it was for his own good. People might go nuts finding him here. Of course, I was joking. No one cares a damn. On our way home, I wanted to chat about India. He said he was tired.

He seemed tired. He got the joke late, believed it, even

though he knew it was a lie. "Lies are all right so long as they're believable." Yes. Wonder how it feels to hear your own jingles played back years later. I'm sure you meant it then. Does it still hold good? I hope so. Truth is, I hate pickup signs. I find them demeaning. I mean to the person whose name is on the sign. Why sell someone out as vain? Anyway, how A. shut me up, I knew I was doing all right, lying.

Waiting is all right, too. You just have to find something. Mom just texted—they put you on a liquid feeding plan. They're not allowing visitors anytime soon. I know you have your cell phone. But I don't want to waste time leaving voice messages you may not hear for days. Besides, Beena K. might come out at any moment and start yelling. Like last night.

They were at a party. I was outside, then she came out flailing her arms, yelling at someone—not A., who was right on her heels. Someone said something at the party about her film—someone called Lisa, who used to live with her. She hit her. Then she sat inside the car, looking straight ahead into the snow, and she wasn't yelling anymore. It was so quiet inside the car, you could hear her breathe, hear my stomach growl over the swish of the wiper blades. Then she fell asleep. Sometime later, when she woke up, her body shook against the seat. She kept whispering as if she had to tell herself to stay solid.

Breathe, swallow. Breathe, swallow. Don't die on me, please, I thought. You can't help thoughts.

Last night, 403 was deserted. It didn't feel the same

looking at the snow. Earlier, I used to feel nostalgic remembering all the shovelling we had to do in Brampton; remembering the time when something happened at your work, and we had just the basement to ourselves and learned that the heating down there was all screwed up, and there was snow in the duct. It was a slow crawl on the highway. She was so wild a minute ago, I kept observing her in the rear-view. Are you all right? I wondered as she took off a glove, touched the edges of her mouth, touched the white V-neck sweater dress she wore, touched the ripped-knee leggings under the camel-brown shearling coat, touched her Medusa wig, now frazzled after the long day, touched the gold pin on the left lapel of her coat, casually revealing the black and purple of her dead husband's brand—WAZZ Films. Something from the past. She kept that, too. She wears it everywhere. Suddenly the storm got worse. We were on the 410 now, dead slow. The car ahead, a black Silverado, had a tail light missing. I remember looking at A., at his dark hat, which contrasted against the snowed window. His face turned away, looking out. You could tell something terrible had happened between them at the party.

The car ahead was braking oddly. Who else was driving in this storm? For a second, I wanted to know, to confirm my intuition—I wasn't the only one fighting a storm. Then the Silverado slowed down, stopped completely. I could see the rotating flashes from the salt truck ahead. Everything came to a standstill.

Right after that, A. cranked up the music as if he wanted to flush out whatever had happened at the party. He had his phone paired to the car stereo. He played Three 6 Mafia. He started singing along, "That's the way the game goes." Then he started slurring. I looked at him.

"Look ahead. Stay in your lane." Beena K. is so protective of A., it's annoying.

The traffic ahead of us had once again ground to a near standstill; a salt truck was doing its thing. She thought I wasn't looking. Her voice, razor-sharp—something I hadn't experienced before. In the rear-view, I could see wiper blades like little arms clearing fuzzy eyes. It was ten after one. Now 6ix9ine was playing. You don't know them.

"This music's hurting my fucking head." Beena K. had cupped her ears with both hands.

I had never heard her swear before. A. tried to sing along: "She wanna fuck, fuck, fuck." It was clear he had a good sense of the beat. I kept driving, you know, for a long time. It felt like a long time. I felt stupid. Beena K. said nothing. A. turned around, grabbed her by the neck and tried to kiss her. His hat fell to the floor as he tried pinning her to the seat. It was hard watching them and watching the road at the same time. I'd have preferred to pull over to the shoulder, let them finish. They were down there for a bit before Beena K. floated back up. I had taken my eyes off the road. The Silverado ahead swung abruptly over to the shoulder and started flashing emergency lights as if trying to show me what I should do. It was half past two. It was slow.

Then A. said something into Beena K.'s ear.

"Show me," she said.

"You sure?" he said.

"Show it," she said, louder this time.

"Forget it. Let's talk about your film. Why don't you want to talk about your film with anyone?" He looked away, his voice gravelly and dry as if he were trying to correct a mistake and had already given up.

"You think you can flake out at will and come back?"

"I didn't flake out. Pitch as if your life depends on it. Do it. Come on."

"Don't be a jerk."

"See, you don't have a proper pitch. You just want to wing it."

"I've already done it."

"They've only read it on paper. Hearing from you is different."

Then Beena K. launched into this story she wants to film: "The main character is a mix of Asifa Bano and Medusa, the Greek Gorgon," she cleared her throat. "AB is working the fields when masked horsemen come and snatch her. AB is taken into a temple. Eight men for eight days rape her. They come to her dressed like gods. They come on high horses. They leave when they're done. They come back. They keep coming. AB is a ruined peach—she's eight or nine or ten—she dies. But her mother—who put her there in the field—is outraged for her being there when these horsemen came. She pins the blame on AB as if she were the one who had called for them. Now Act Two. The mother disowns AB. No one would bury her. Her body disappears. Now AB is the snake-locked Medusa, hanging down from mulberry trees, haunting the country, waiting for revenge. But who would she go after? The gods who came on high horses? Or the mother who disowned her? The townsfolk know the story—they worry about retribution; they think there will be war. But there is no war. Instead, an ecstasy pervades the country like an enchanting song. A song so enchanting, you must shut your ears, or it'll take you in its power. Those who pay no heed are taken, sucked inside a cave where they meet others taken like them. This cave looks like Plato's cave—dark, and you face a wall and behind you there is fire, and on the parapet there are puppeteers. But you can turn your head; you can see a crack of light at the far side from where this ecstasy-song pours into you. The song draws you in like a rare-earth magnet. It has absolute power over you. The inmates of the cave keep moving towards this crack from where this ecstasy-song pours in, chained to each other in a single file, holding onto the shoulders of the man ahead. Closer they get to this ecstasy-crack, they feel it; the drug-like power of the song makes them blind. Everyone in the cave is in its spell. Everyone is blind. They don't see the puppeteers on the parapet performing for them. They don't need to see the fire. One by one, the whole town is gone, then the valley. Police, military, clergy, the whole country look for the dark cave. Those who can't hear the song never find the cave. Those who hear the song, can't resist the cave. And when far too many are lost, those who are left behind, pin it on AB. They begin to fear her. She's cast in stone like Ahalya, the eternal infidel. Then they make a temple so they can appease her, and in the temple, they draw a thousand labia-shaped eyes, so they never forget her."

A. let out a chuckle. Beena K. darted a glance at A. Then he burst into laughter as if to fill the void in the car with something more familiar.

"What?" she hit him playfully.

"That's a long pitch."

A couple of police cars were stationed on the shoulder of the highway, doing nothing. The red and blue from their beacon flashes fell on the road slick from the ice the plow couldn't scrape out.

"It's a long film."

"You're damned right. Since you want to make movies no one else wants to make, this one would be it." A. said, before pulling her towards him and kissing her passionately.

After a while, she said, "Stop." Beena K. moved away.

"We just got started."

"I don't like it."

"What's wrong?"

"Why won't anyone else want to make it?" Beena K. slid back close. He started cuddling her. The cars ahead had started moving at a clip.

"Because that's not how it happened. Because if you lie

about something like that, they'll come after you; they'll drag you inside the cave, ask you to bend over and—bam—a budding filmmaker shot in the ass. And that would be the final take on that."

"Truth doesn't matter. Feelings matter. That's how I feel and I'm going to make it."

"No, you won't."

"You're scared?"

"Wouldn't you be? Except that, after the film is made, you'll stay back here for the ceremonies, awards, and seminars; you'll make the fancy speeches. What would I do? I have to head back home."

"Why?"

"What do you mean 'why?'"

"I can't imagine I'm sitting next to a chicken locked inside a man's body."

A. looked out of the window, then turned sharply to face Beena K. "Here, now listen to my pitch."

"You don't have a pitch," she said.

"I just made it up. It'll take a minute."

"I don't care. You're not here to pitch. You're here to help me make my film."

"What if I have an alternative story?"

"Alternative to what?"

"Don't you have one minute?"

She didn't reply, so he started.

"Consider this character—Q. She's chasing Karla. Q. is you. Karla is a serial killer's lover. They had this on the gangster series last night, that's how I know Karla. But you're from here, you know her already."

"Turn it off." Beena K. pointed at his phone.

"Calm down."

She looked in the mirror to check what I was doing.

"The movie starts after Karla's out of jail. She has gone missing. She has changed her name. But someone spots her at a childcare centre in a small town. It's all over the papers."

"How does she look? Pretty? I need a picture in my head."

"We don't know. They got a profile shot. The town is close to the U.S. border. They have tonnes of strangers in that town. They can't believe a serial killer could come to live with them. Not until they see this ad in the papers requesting information about Karla, the pretty monster. Now they're sure Karla is there. Q. placed the ad because Karla is her story. Fifty dollars for any leads on Karla. This has everyone in town worried about everyone. But something else happens. Act Two."

A truck sped out of nowhere, splattering the windscreen with slush. Then we passed Bramalea. At last, we were moving.

"That's enough." Beena K. cupped her ears again. She doesn't want to play.

"Q. starts getting calls from the townsfolk. Q. meets informers, she pays the price, they feed her stories. Oh! We saw Karla at the church, at the cemetery, at the theatre, outside the school. Yes, Karla was with a teenager. Yes, she was kissing someone very, very young. She's the pretty monster who has returned. Then the stories begin to contradict each other. Now Q. is not sure what to believe. She realizes she has been taken. And then the real Karla shows up at a grocery store with someone, say, a fat sucker. And she's no longer pretty, just old. And she's no longer menacing, just quaint: No longer a monster, and Q. can't do Karla anymore."

"What's your point?"

"You don't know AB. That's not your story."

"What do you know about what I know?"

"Pick the other one. The four-act *Bildungsroman*—climax and then something else. Do what you know. Here, let me read it. *A cute brown girl wakes up one day to find both her parents gone in the crash of Flight 182. Cute girl finds out she's bisexual when a woman in the foster family touches her, and they go down a spiral. The girl finds who she really is, then a cancer diagnosis gives her a double mastectomy, then the girl finds out she's in a marriage triangle involving her movie-mogul husband and his ex with 48E breasts, then she plots revenge, and something happens to the car they're driving, and the husband is dead, and the girl becomes suspect number one, but she clears her name, eventually.*"

"I don't want that story anymore. The grant is for AB."

"Of course, you do. You had me read it."

"You changed the subject because you got scared. You flaked out. That's the truth."

"I didn't flake out."

"I'd believe you if this was the only time."

"Everything would be okay if I was coming to you now?"

"It's humiliating. Just fucking stay awake."

"Can we just pull over?" A. said.

"Are you talking to me?" I asked.

"Yes. Please. Sir," A. said. "Pull over on the shoulder here."

"Keep driving," Beena K. said. It looked like she had had enough. She looked exhausted.

"Right here," he rolled down the windows.

"Keep going." Beena K. forced him away as he tried sliding close to her again, her wrist striking his face. Then she began to cry. Then they remained silent for a while before he managed to slide back up and put his arm around her again. And they remained like that.

The roads were finally clearing. I exited the 410, now on the final stretch. No one said another word. I slipped quietly into a line of cars built up at the ramp heading to Heart Lake.

After a while, I saw them kissing again. Passionately. Like Chekhov's Gurov, kissing the lady with the little dog. She said nothing, but darted a glance at me as though it were not my place to look at them making out. I noticed she opened her bag, popped another pill—must be Percocet. He dragged her down again.

"Stop," she said.

"What's wrong? Don't you want it?" he whispered, letting her go.

She said nothing, only looked to make sure I wasn't watching. I looked ahead at the ice-pelted side roads, hating it inside the car, not knowing what to do. My eyes were popping out. My throat dry, a stabbing ache shooting through the right side of my body. I couldn't bear driving anymore. I knew I had to hurry. So I started driving faster. I looked out the window. The storm was dead quiet between the dark windows on either side of the high-rent neighbourhood.

They went down again.

"Stop," she yelled again. And it was no plain shout—a shriek, incoherent, laced with venom, rising from the depth of her belly. He was doing something to her I couldn't see. Perhaps sliding his hands up her shirt in a manner she didn't want. Perhaps holding her chest in a manner she didn't want.

I wanted to see what he was doing, but it was dark.

"Stop. Stop. Stop." She didn't want him touching something. A scar. I don't know. Then she struck his body with force, and he let go.

"You don't want it then?"

"You do that again, I'll have you thrown out of the car."

"Is that what you want tonight?"

Beena K. kept her fists drawn, ready to strike if he came close.

"Is that how you want it? In a heap?" He tried once more to take her hand in his, leaning in to draw his face closer to hers. She seemed cross about whatever he had done earlier. I don't know. I had never seen her this mad. She hit him again, on his chest, harder this time. And then something got to him—his face shook, his jaw clenched tight, his teeth drawn out like an animal gone rabid. Fat, twisted veins popped up on his forehead. He enlarged himself like a monster, grabbed her, dug his fingers deep into her neck, deep and hard, until she was lost in the dark under his body. It seemed as though he were taking her right there.

At first, I thought it was a gag—that he'd stop, unfreeze, let go at any moment—and it would end in a laugh. Until he kept going into her, I think, forcing himself deeper, so it seemed. For a bit, I didn't hear anything. It happened so fast I didn't know if I should stop, do something.

Then I saw her fending him off, striking him viciously with her legs, hands, digging her nails into his flesh through the unbuttoned shirt.

I kept watching, then I pressed the gas and let the car gather speed in the slick so I could swing it off the street and ratchet into the snowbank before spinning back. The car scuffed past a parked Cherokee on the curb.

"Fuck!" they both yelled, as I waited for the vehicle to stop spinning.

"Watch the fucking road," Beena K. said.

I stopped the engine before rolling the window down to check the damage. The sharp chill slammed into my face.

"Turn. Turn. Turn," she said, leaning over, trying to look past the dark. My car was facing the opposite way. "It's nothing," she said. "Just turn around, and we'll be fine."

When we reached Beena K.'s home, she had to wobble her way up the long driveway to the main entrance. I reasoned it was because she was drunk. Or something was with her new dress shoes, or something had happened to her.

"Are you alright?" I asked.

When she didn't respond, I asked again. She turned and stared at me. And I turned to stone. She didn't say another word. I said nothing more. Watched her fumble at the door, taking her sweet time to slide the key into the hole. Then she stood like a ghost under the door frame, waiting for A. to walk up to her, and then she slammed the door shut on his face, so close it must have got his nose.

I didn't know what else to do. I waited. I saw him banging on the door, working the doorbell, his phone, blowing steam into his gloved hands. He kicked the door a couple of times. Then he ran back to the waiting car, back to where he had sat earlier.

"What are you looking at?" he said. "Let's go."

"Where now?"

"Just drive."

And then I drove him here. To this hotel. And I don't know why, somehow, I knew I had to get back to Beena K. I dropped him off and drove up to her house. As I waited, I looked around into the snow-lit street—calm, serene, undisturbed. At the far end of the crescent, I could see the flicker of moving images on a dark window, someone else was awake. I saw a frayed wreath stuck to her door from the holidays, plastic and firmly positioned. It was half past three.

For a moment I thought I'd call Faye, then I wondered, what if Beena K. opened the doors right then, what would I say to her? Did I have something to say? In a few hours, it'd be morning. I knew that. I headed back home. Mom said I should have stayed. She said I should have stayed and resisted. Not resisting is chicken. She should know that. I never stayed for her either. Or resisted. I shouldn't be bringing it up now. I feel I had to.

Mom says they were able to get you fresh clothes. They're not allowing anyone past the front desk. Not even she can see you. Hope everything will be all right by tomorrow. Hope they let her in. Me, too. I'll bring Grandma's cheese-cake from that store in Lorne Park. You might want it.

Now inside the car, the cranked-up heat has fogged the windows, everything's gone fuzzy. The lot is empty. Through the snow, the hotel entrance shines. There is no one there. Everyone's home. Wonder if this is it or if there will be another storm. Wonder how much longer they'll keep you. The spring-head dog on the dashboard just moved. Beena K. hasn't called yet. But she might. She didn't want me to stop waiting. I want to walk inside, find out. Maybe they're fucking. Who knows who's fucking who? I'll find out eventually. Faye will tell me what's going on. It's late now. Mom will tell me how to go about the visit tomorrow. Everything will be fine tomorrow.

2019

SHULUT

The Blue Skies of Stoney Creek

"Hear that?" Rono turned onto his side, looked at the closed door through the haze of the mosquito net, and fell back on the bed, staring at the ceiling. It was August. The smell of dampness fanned the walls. Yellow paint flaked like scales. Beyond the rain and the ceiling fan, nothing. Not a sound. He needed to go to the bathroom but didn't want to get out of bed yet. Not until he could see at least a sliver of light stream through the craggy edges of the window. Just to be sure the night was finally over.

Rubina didn't answer. Just a little while back, the clock had struck five. He knew she was awake. He knew she'd be in bed at least an hour longer. He knew what she wanted. As he turned onto his side again to look at the door, Rono could feel the sheets moving with him, stuck to his body, damp with sweat. His throat felt dry. He was having a hard time keeping his hands from shaking. He had been out of whisky for a whole week.

The village hooch hut would open again after ten, like every day. He hated the look of the new fatso who had taken over. "I don't keep Tiger," the man had said. Tiger was the only country spirit Rono's stomach could take, even though it looked like piss. He knew that colour. He had seen it in his grandfather's bedpan for years. They had Blue; he could be dead drinking that stuff, like the ones who choked on their own vomit two summers back. He hadn't been here in Shulut when that happened; he had heard and tried it anyway.

The main bazaar was less than two miles from Shulut, a dusty farm town of a few hundred houses, fifty miles west of Calcutta. Nothing ever happened in Shulut other than puja and the vote—federal, state, council. The vote came in cycles, like a prolonged menstruation, shedding blood with cramping pain, leaving behind hope. The civic vote had just come and gone. That was June. Puja wasn't until October, a wait of three months before something would happen. But then, a week after the vote, Dulal was hanged, and three weeks later, officers from the district took Bishu Sen away. God knows where. And now this mark on his own house.

Not long ago, it took him less than twenty minutes by bicycle to reach the bazaar liquor store, two blocks from the police station. Ever since the vote, this short distance took him an hour. He knew something was wrong. Every time he got on his bike, his muscles froze; a stabbing pain choked him. Maybe it had something to do with the way he was sitting on the bike, Rubina had said. How could that be? He could hear it right now, the slow clatter of his teeth, even though Rubina was right by his side on the bed. He knew she was up. He knew she didn't want to talk about the mark. He knew he needed to keep his hands still. He tried holding on to the bed frame, hoping the shivers would go away.

It hadn't always been like this. Nine months back, when he got to Shulut, his only fear was getting kicked out of this house he had stolen into. Not his house. Nor the land at the other end of town—all forty acres of it that now belonged to his maternal uncles back in Calcutta. "What about me?" he asked. But by then his mother had given up on possessions and had followed her guru to Benares. She didn't want to be part of this. He was fourteen then, afraid to challenge her. But the more he stayed in Shulut, the more he found out—there were other things to be afraid of: kraits, scorpions, ghosts, spells, kinsmen, and now this mark, a left-handed swastika out of nowhere. What was he going to do about it? Six weeks ago, it had seemed like a dumb prank. Not anymore. Not after it showed up every day this week.

"You forgot to put the pot under the leak. The floor's all wet," he said.

"I got it down last night. I need it in the kitchen," Rubina replied, moving closer to his body, pressing her breasts against his naked shoulder blades, startling him as she grazed the back of his neck with her dry lips.

He wasn't ready to be touched yet. "Why? What's happening in the kitchen?"

"Why can't you get the leak fixed?"

How did he forget? It had been over a month since he'd stepped out of the house.

"Don't worry about it all the time." She pressed against him harder now, caressing his belly.

"Don't."

"Why? Don't I have needs?"

"My bladder will explode."

"Then why don't you go to the bathroom?"

"It's raining. What happened to your ears?"

"Rain, no rain, what difference does it make?" Rubina asked, still holding him, touching him again under the belly.

"Was I sick again?" He shook her off.

"Toru's coming to lunch. She might have news from Bishu Sen." She moved away.

Toru used to be Bishu Sen's mistress, a few houses down the alley at Number 14. Rono used to visit Bishu Sen every Saturday. One of the few weekly rituals he looked forward to ever since they got here. Not anymore.

Rono slid out from beneath the mosquito net, dragged himself to the door, and stood waiting. Then he took a deep breath, as if he needed to draw up extra strength to get the wood jammer off the door. Outside, hurrying past the flies hovering over his vomit, pinching his nose as the acid smell hit him, he took long strides, his feet splashing on the unpaved corridor to the bathroom.

The rain had stopped, but the ground was still wet. Patches of light had broken through the grey sky, reflected on dark puddles in the dirt. Even the faintest drift in the leaves—mango, papaya, jackfruit, fig—slammed his chest, and the stabbing shot back up like a current, hitting his head, travelling down his neck, past the shoulder, down the spine, burning his calves and the arches of his feet. It surprised him that Rubina hadn't cleaned up last night. The sight of his own vomit disgusted him. Then he started looking for the mark. Better him than anyone else.

The first time it had appeared—spray-painted on the unplastered outer building of the estate, he ignored it. Perhaps an angry farmhand punching back, he thought. Three days later, he found it again, drawn in quick brush strokes on the weather-beaten kitchen door across the courtyard. Next, it was hidden under a cloud of mosquitoes on a handbill nailed to the door of the squat toilet by the outer building. Then he found it painted on a tin can hung like a pendant on the neck of the hand pump, out in the yard.

Perhaps a game. For a while, the wrong-facing swastikas showed up only weekly. Last week, when the mark showed up every day, he knew it was something else—perhaps a message. He hoped someone could tell him how to read it.

Every time he found the mark, he scraped, washed, ripped it off, painted it over. He got rid of it as fast as he could and with great secrecy, as if it were his fault. As if the random popping-up of a familiar mark had transformed it into a terrible portent, and he was somehow responsible. He didn't want anyone to know. But then it showed up repeatedly, at regular intervals, like a chronic rash; he had to rush inside and drag Rubina out of bed, as if he needed help to understand what it was. The next few times, he did the same, dragging her from wherever she was, and they faced the mark together as if he expected her to know where it came from, what it was about. Together they had looked at the mark with a mix of awe and dread. But the marks kept coming, new marks at predictable intervals, like the pendulum of a giant clock.

Over the last six weeks, he noticed Rubina's interest in them petering out. She refused to be drawn into the ritual of deciphering. Last week, even though the mark had shown up every day, Rubina hadn't even bothered to look, as if she knew—as if someone had told her—what they were, why they were coming—as if she had made her peace with what she knew.

"It's here," Rono said, darting up the porch steps into the darkness of the large bedroom in the two-storey row house—a room to each storey—connected by a cement stairway near the door.

"Where?" Rubina raised herself in the bed as he walked over to the dresser, looking for something. In the mirror, past his own head of curly dark hair, he could see the contours of her forehead curved like a coffee bean, the flourish of her pointy nose, the long braid of black hair trailing her head, large cinnamon eyes following every movement of his hand encroaching her domain. The cracks in the window beside her had started to break out. In that faint light, he had a hard time looking through. His hairy hands—so large he had difficulty fitting them in the pockets of his pyjamas—dismantling her little possessions on top of the dresser. He looked at her again. She didn't look twenty-one. He didn't look thirty-eight. Ever since she had gotten pregnant, she looked older. Perhaps even happier. At least she laughed more often. Of course, she had made her peace here in Shulut, this septic, middle-of-nowhere town. That disgusted him.

"Is it the wrong one again?" She flopped back on the bed, turning away, back towards the window. She seemed to be smiling—the wry smile of someone knowing something terrible has happened again and is helpless before it. He knew she wouldn't get out of the bed to check it out. It wasn't yet time. He didn't answer. He simply pointed his face to the new mark he had found outside, flame-burnt to the wooden door frame.

There were a dozen other houses in B-Col—a back alley zigzagging all the way from the outer building, through No. 1, where Rono lived, tapering out like the neck of a water sewer, thirteen houses deep into a bamboo thicket, before spreading into a mango grove and then a fishpond, facing house No. 14, the circular three-storey brick house of Bishu Sen, the top dog of the Sen clan until they took him away.

Rono's twice-removed grand-uncles and -aunts and a clutch of country cousins lived in these row houses—Nos. 2 to 13—right up to the thicket, each house touching the next, each uniquely patchy with paint peeling like blisters. They looked similar—cousins, uncles, and aunts—brushed in the same shade of caramel. They shared the same water from the lone tube well. They had fish and rice for lunch and a nap right after. They spoke in slightly different dialects about the same set of things. Yet the mark had shown up nowhere else. Why was it him alone?

Haru seemed to have an explanation. Haru, of all people. A ganja-smoking Baul with a black tongue and a taste for dark predictions that usually turned out right. Rono knew him—a harmless dimwit, creature of the wild, either sprawled on the cement bench at the bus station or hiding in the brushwood behind the corner store all day, only to appear in the afternoon just past lunch hour—singing the same set of Baul songs in a low pitch, shaking his head over his scrawny frame covered in a patchwork of garments knotted in the shape of one huge cape—collecting leftovers from the housewives of B-Col, so he could carry them to his lair and eat.

"Who is it?" Rono was ready to believe anything.

"Vote ghosts," Haru said with a wobble of his head. "You can see them every night, hanging down this tree and that one." He was dead serious as the folks gathered around him burst out laughing. "You don't trust me? Come out with me tonight. I'll show you."

"Why is it only me?" Rono thought Haru might know.

"Would it make you feel better if the mark was on our house instead of yours?" someone in the crowd had shouted out.

"Someone who?" Rubina wanted to know later on. But Rono didn't know the person's name. He had no interest in the names of his grand-uncles and -aunts, cousins, and kinsfolk who lived beside him in B-Col's narrow, conjoined houses—twice-removed maternal relatives he knew nothing of until nine months back when he had first arrived. He had known they existed somewhere in the back alleys of a faraway country. He thought of them just as he had been warned by his uncles in Calcutta—kraits, scorpions, thugs, whores. Stay away from them.

Rono tried scraping the mark off the door frame with a rusty chisel, but it was cut deep, and the blunt chisel was useless. He went back into the house for a fresh supply of implements. On his way in, he ran his finger over the mark. For a second, he considered whether he should mask it with dirt and forget about it. But the door was the colour of bergamot. Rubina had gotten him to paint it fresh. Reaching into his toolbox, he looked for sandpaper.

After a brief spell of sun, the clouds had trooped back in, an eerie darkness taking over. This sudden drop in the heat eased his nerves. He liked the sky dark. It gave him a degree of cover so he could do his job. It could be a mistake after all. He looked around occasionally to see if anyone was watching. He worked the sandpaper on the door frame until the naked seam of the wood became visible.

He could see Rubina's head bobbing under the low window of the kitchen as she ate her breakfast alone. She got hungry often. He understood. He wasn't hungry yet. He watched her walk back across the narrow, unpaved courtyard into the house, stopping briefly to check the results of his toil. Inside, she looked at the dressing mirror, took her sweet time to straighten her hair, knot it in a highball, fix the folds of her saree, rip a red velvet bindi off the spotty mirror and stick it between her groomed eyebrows before settling in with a cup of tea, milky and syrupy sweet. He liked it raw and bitter. Something about her was grating on his nerves.

"You just made it worse," she said, letting out a loud slurp from the teacup.

"What do you want?"

"Leave it alone. It's nothing."

"I'm going to paint it over."

"Where would you get paint? You haven't left the house in weeks."

"I'm going to use your nail polish."

"No, you're not." Without saying another word, Rubina stormed out to the kitchen.

Rono found the bottle of mustard-yellow lacquer hidden deep inside the drawers of her dressing table and worked it with the brush into the naked patch on the door frame. As he tried to put the cap back on the bottle, his hand shook and the bottle crashed, spilling some of its contents onto the cement of the porch where his vomit was.

Later, when he noticed Rubina return with a broom and phenyl to clean it up, he felt a mix of pity, fear, and loathing. He had a feeling someone was watching him. Watching them. No one told him that, but he knew. He knew someone had to be always watching, as he was watching, not so long ago, Dulal's body—limp and heavy—up on the electrical tower near the highway. It had stayed hung the whole day, taking in the rain. They all watched as the police brought it down from the height. Watched as an army of newsmen with cameras and headphones came invading, in waves, like locusts, talking torrentially into the camera beyond the stunned watchers, urging them to "tell us what you saw. Tell us what happened." But no one had seen anything. No one had anything to say. No one except Bishu Sen.

"Council vote is over. It'll come back, but Dulal is gone. We're not even the same party. He was orange. I'm not orange. He believed in God. I believe in men. He sold country hooch out of his store, out of his home, out of the temple. I'm a revolutionary. But our blood is the same colour. Our sweat has the same salt. Should we accept this as bad luck? Or fight back? I know they're watching. I know. They think they've taken everything. They think they've left us nothing to fight back with. Not even words. They're mistaken. We'll find the words. The words are buried in our hearts. I don't believe in the soul. We'll find the heart. We must find the heart, the words, and fight back. If not words, then what? If not now, when?" Bishu Sen looked straight into the camera, his voice unwavering, his head still as everyone around him shuffled uneasily, looking down into the dirt. They didn't want him speaking. Not for them at least. But no one stopped him.

The same afternoon, the newsmen left, trailing the

police van that carried Dulal's body to the district for post-mortem. They said they'd come back for the inquest. Later that night, Rono had stayed glued to the TV, surfing channels, so he could show Rubina what Bishu Sen had said to the reporters. Rono liked what Bishu Sen had said. When he couldn't find it on the news, he enacted the scene for Rubina, repeating every word, pausing frequently for the right intonation. But when they came back for Bishu Sen, Rono wasn't there. Hungover in his bed, he had failed again. It grated on him. He knew he'd be next.

Every Saturday, Rono visited Bishu Sen, without an invite, of his own accord. It had started out of curiosity. Bishu Sen, the polestar of the Sen clan! He used to be a college professor in Calcutta. He returned to the country a few years back, after his wife died. With both his sons in America, with his own college tenure over, his political work reduced to condolence meetings behind closed doors, he quietly made his way back to his ancestral house, expecting to retire. And then he became legally blind, losing first his left eye to a fudged cataract operation and then his right to the fear of another mishap, even though his vision had ripened to the point where he said, "Every object in a formless yellow world is now fused into everything else."

Rono remembered standing on the second-floor balcony of Bishu Sen's circular house—the exterior painted all white; cornices, headers, trims, painted in a rich shade of red. He remembered the uneasy excitement the first time he stood there on the balcony, looking at the courtyard below, at the mango grove beyond, then the clump of bamboo trees, and then, far off, the scabby, uneven masonry, the rain-battered exteriors of houses 1 to 13. It felt as if his own standing among kinsfolk had gotten a boost merely by his being there on Bishu Sen's balcony. Those moments he was there, looking down at the rest of B-Col, he no longer felt like an outsider. It was as if he had his foot firmly on the machine. He could control it; he had found his cruising altitude, right at the top.

When they met, the evenings unfolded in a pattern, starting with Bishu Sen staring at the TV, not uttering a word as if, denied the privilege of sight, he was reconstructing his perception of the world through the world news. His cataract, he said, was "a natural filter. Good, bad, ugly—everything needs to be sieved and sifted and seeped before letting it hit the mind's eye, the third eye. That's all you have. If that gets cataracted, you're gone."

Rono felt privileged to participate in this quiet osmosis and ascribed it, beyond his bloodline, to his ability to stay speechless for long periods without letting his presence be known. He was happy Bishu Sen had taken him into his small circle of privilege—retired teachers, poets, ousted officials, diehard country apparatchiks who, like Bishu Sen, quietly listened to the news of the world, in rapt attention, sipping on raw-red tea and bitter. When the cycle of news started to feel repetitive, they left, just as quietly as they had appeared. The first time that happened, Rono had taken it as an accident; when the same thing repeated, he could sense the pattern. He realized it had to do with him.

Allowed the privilege of approach, perhaps he hadn't been accorded access. For access into the innermost sanctum of this secret Comintern, there were perhaps rites of passage. He wasn't aware. So hanging on to the thread of his bloodline, without a word, he waited for the moment, late into each evening, when Bishu Sen, assured that all the apparatchiks were gone, would press a buzzer. Toru's shadow would appear behind the wooden cabinetry where his imported whisky was hidden. Ice would follow. Bishu Sen would give instructions for her to bring the fritters she had been getting ready all evening just for this after-meeting. They drank quietly, still looking at the TV, as the realization slowly crept into Rono's head: Bishu Sen had pegged him in the same category as the "common folk of B-Col."

"But I'm not them." Rono would look at Bishu Sen when addressing him.

"How so?"

"I'm an artist. You see? Not the commissar you make me out to be."

"And what kind of art do you do?"

"I make sculptures."

"And what's your material?"

"Metal shavings from lathe factories."

"Sculptures from trash. Aha! And what do you make? Gods and toys?"

"Busts and mannequins."

"Statues? Do you make statues?"

"I haven't made one cast since I got here."

"There is always a start. You can start with mine. A copper statue that will become green with time, out in the courtyard."

"You mean like the Statue of Liberty?"

"Yes, but this would be the Statue of Persistence. Or maybe the Statue of Trial."

And so his visits became more frequent, and he no longer seemed like a fringe groupie; he was an equal, participating in something that might outlive them both, something that might become something—a symbol for the hundred years of the Sens of Shulut.

"And where did you say your studio was?"

"Kimber Street in Calcutta. It used to be a lathe shop."

"And who was buying?"

"Gina Farini. All of it. My sole patron. My singular buyer."

"And who's Gina Farini?"

"Auro's new wife. He brought her to my studio once when they came visiting Calcutta. Must be a couple of years back, two years and some months. She came to my studio, in a sleeveless top and trousers that stopped at the knee. What a distraction! Everyone kept ogling her body, but her eyes were on me. Whatever I showed her—moulded, carved, cast, assembled; abstracts, rounds, relief; copper, aluminum, iron—she liked them all, every piece on display. She wanted them all. She took them all. All of it, all the way to Stoney Creek."

"Stoney Creek?" Bishu Sen winced at the hard bite of bone in the batter-fried tilapia that Toru had brought in once and refilled again just to keep them busy while she cooked dinner.

Rono explained Stoney Creek as he knew it, as he had seen it inside a hand-held camcorder. "Let's just say one huge field of flowers, all yellow. And the land, not like here, split into squares like a one-tone ludo board. It's one huge piece of earth, nothing to stop the dice from rolling from this end to that end of the sky, as far as the eye can see. One piece of flat under a gigantic roof as though you were a child inside a clear glass dome. In the darkened sky, the moon looks so big; if you stretch hard from your terrace, I'm sure you can touch it. It's that close. I touched it and the frame inside the camera moved. Blue skies everywhere, and the land—nothing to stop it from rolling on and on and on, golden with corn, ready for picking. Not a soul anywhere, just earth and sky. A sea of gold, interrupted by toy houses where no one lives. A different kind of gold. The clouds, the sky, the trees with metal leaves—green, yellow, brown, red. Not the red you see here, not the green outside the balcony, a different kind of blue, that sky. I wish I could show you."

"There is nothing to see. I've seen it all."

"Aurobindo—Uncle Visma's son, you know him—he's the one who's the lawyer in Stoney Creek; his wife, she's the special one, you should have seen her. She was a secretary before she became an art collector. She's Italian. Her skin, white like birdlime, sweet entrapment, with so many spots, so many, you'd think someone sprayed bronze dust on her face just to make it look brown. But her hands and legs and neck and shoulders, those were all red. She said, 'Come with us.' Auro stayed quiet. Perhaps he didn't approve. He's the quiet type. But Gina, she was excited; she wanted me to pack my bags right then, bring the show to Stoney Creek. They'd love my work there, she said. I deserve to be up there, she said. Up there in Stoney Creek and Halifax where she was born."

"Did you know Leon Trotsky was in Halifax just before the revolution—dragged off the ship to Russia and hauled into a prison camp."

"Three copper Buddhas and a sea horse in silicon bronze. She took them to Stoney Creek. I gave everything for free the first time. I'm an artist, you see, not a businessman. Auro insisted on paying. I refused. He's the weird one. Why take money from someone who gives you something you've never had, something you can only dream about."

"And what was that?"

"A bottle of ice-wine and a window seat on a plane," Rono laughed. "It was believable then. I could believe anything in those days. I used to be a different man. Not this one you see here. This one is an imposter, a ghost in another man's skin. It was a different time, altogether a different time in history, a time so different, so different, just a couple of years back. I flew my work across the oceans. I knew everyone; everyone knew me."

"Everyone knows you here." Bishu Sen adjusted his weight on the divan as Rono poured him more whisky.

"Here in Shulut? I don't know anyone. Not a soul. But everyone knows me. They know everything about me. They know I'm here with you now. They know what we're drinking. They know the colour of the shit I'm going to crap out tomorrow." Rono nodded at Toru to take the empty plates away.

Bishu Sen shook his head and chortled, almost choking as he popped the last fritter. Staring at the TV, glassy-eyed, he didn't seem in the mood to listen anymore. "You know what Trotsky did when they shoved him inside a prison camp?"

Rono kept silent. He wasn't sure. He had never heard that name before.

"He started converting German prisoners into commies, and then they let him go," Bishu Sen slurred, before letting his droopy eyelids close completely. Never mind if Rono went on, like filler, in between the stages of his sleep, telling him how, two years back, the same week he was to make his trip to Stoney Creek, he had suffered a stroke; how his right hand—his working hand—stopped moving for a time; how the doctor looked him in the eye and said, "That's it;" and how Rubina brought him back from the verge of suicide with a bottle of voodoo; how she massaged his frozen hand for hours every afternoon; how one accident led to another, all the way to Shulut.

Bishu Sen raised himself on the divan with a start, sometimes nodding uninterestedly as Rono told him how the whole Sen clan came screaming at him once their affair became public—an affair with the housemaid. After that, he had no choice. So here he was in Shulut, but not before he grabbed Rubina's hand and walked her around a firepit, not before he had done the only honourable thing left for him to do.

"So you saved her?" Bishu Sen said after a prolonged silence, uttering each word with a carefully modulated pause. As Rono leaned over the polished teak table to pour the last drop of whisky into his glass, "Or she saved you?"

Rono didn't know how to respond to that one. He knew the truth was half and half—like whisky, you add the water to stoke the flavour before the water takes the whisky—takes it, flattens it, drowns it, and you can't drink it anymore. Maybe that's what he'd say to Bishu Sen. He waited for him to wake up.

But now Bishu Sen was gone. They had taken him. And the clock struck twelve. As he looked towards the sky, the sun hurt his eyes. The shadows were twisted into each other like metal rods. He saw Rubina in the kitchen, her face radiant in the steam as she removed the lid from a boiling pot. Must be rice. He wasn't hungry. He stepped out to the porch and slumped, his legs melting in the heat. He felt his vision blur, come back, then blur again suddenly into complete darkness as if a dodgy bulb had gone bust inside his brain. He dragged himself inside, but his hands shook as if in seizure, and he veered off balance, slumping again onto the bedroom floor. He stayed sprawled on the ground before lifting himself back up on the bed. He crawled on the bed towards the window, which Rubina always kept shut. He knew he needed a drink. He struggled with the rusty barrel bolt on the window before realizing Rubina had jammed it with coir rope. Through the closed window, he pictured himself walking the mile along the river road to the hooch hut under a red umbrella, a freckled white hand holding it out for him. But no matter how long he walked, the hooch hut remained the same distance away.

When he woke up, he felt something in his throat wrenching the air out, and Rubina's big toenail dug into his bare arm. He looked at her. As she smiled, he went back down with a gasp. Staring at the ceiling, he pictured the mark in the rust-coloured water stains around the corners of the ceiling. He knew the mark. He had seen it countless times since childhood, painted on door frames in every room at his grandfather's house in Calcutta. He knew the four hands of the swastika framed the four corners of an imaginary square. He felt different about those hands back then, always pointing right, always moving clockwise if you looked at them for a while. But the hands here, they faced the wrong way, moved wrong. These, too. The ones painted by rain, just like the ones outside.

He looked at Rubina slouched on the bed, crocheting a blanket. Absently, he started stroking her feet—dyed around the edges with alta that had faded—occasionally turning the silver blob on her index toe ring halfway, as if it were a bolt knob and he needed to turn it to find his way in.

"Where have they taken him? Did Toru tell you?"

"Taken whom?"

"Didn't you ask her about Bishu Sen?"

"She said you owed her husband unpaid wages."

"I knew there was something."

"Why don't you pay?"

"I don't owe her anything. Her husband worked for the company. My uncles are the company. She should go ask them."

"But *you* hired him."

"I haven't been paid either. I'm going to the city tomorrow to collect."

"Why tomorrow?"

"Saturdays are best. Everyone's home. They need to be together, in one place, before they can decide anything."

"What's to decide? I can't be here alone all day."

"How about I drop you off at your sister's?"

"Not there."

"She still thinks her husband has a thing for you? You're pregnant now. Didn't you tell her that?"

Rubina didn't answer.

"Better you stay here," Rono said. "You might get lost in the city, Bi. What would I do then?"

"Why would I get lost?"

"People get lost all the time. You know I can't take you back to the house."

"Didn't you tell them about us? Didn't you tell them we're married?"

"They know. But to stir up old stuff? Who needs that now?"

"Then I won't step out of here. And you stay here, too."

"I need to go. I need to get paid. We need to get out."

"I'm not staying here alone."

"You're not scared. Are you scared, Bi?"

"No. I just don't want to be alone."

"Why doesn't the mark scare you? You think you know what it is?"

Rubina stayed quiet.

"What if you're wrong?" Rono asked.

"About what?"

"About everything. What if it's not the vote ghosts making these marks? What if someone's watching us?"

"Who's watching us?"

"I don't know," Rono said. "You feel someone's always watching. We should pack up. Get the hell out. Go somewhere else."

"Where?"

"Someplace that doesn't choke you every time you step out of your room for air."

"Who's choking you?"

"Someplace with no family. No history."

"What's wrong with history?"

"History's like a yoke; your hands are chained to its ends. You don't see it. But it hangs around your neck, pulling you down until you're ground back into the dirt. Back where you started."

"How do you know when you can't see it?"

"You'll find it if you look."

"History starts the moment you're in a place."

"But that's still a start. People make new starts. We can

make a new start. Being here, chained to this thing, it has made us sick . . . you, me . . . it has spared no one. Don't you see that?"

"I don't see anything in this heat. We need a new fridge."

"Why?"

"Because it's hot. Because my history started here."

"But you don't know anyone here. You hate it here."

"You start. You drink the water. And then you turn and you become one of them, and then you respect their rules, and then there is no hate. Hate empties out. Like this," Rubina said, drinking the last bit from the metal cup close to her and turning it over.

"Respect other people's rules? Why? That's not respect, that's like losing a disc in the spine."

"Every place has rules. Everyone knows that."

"I don't know that, Bi. I don't want to turn. I don't want it."

"No one here has ever told you what to do."

"What's the mark telling us then? What's it telling you?"

Rubina didn't answer. Rono lit another cigarette, the last in the pack. He'd need more, he thought, throwing the empty pack with all his strength, hoping for it to carom off the wall onto the table where his lunch was.

"Get out and smoke," she said.

He stubbed it out in the water from the upturned glass, kept it for later.

By six, the sun had moved from behind the terrace of Bishu Sen's house. The unpaved road outside the entrance to

B-Col still burned in a quiet afterglow. Everything still. Except the smoke rising from Rono's cigarette. He seemed too distracted to smoke. An uneasy calm choked the leaves of the fig tree that loomed over the outer building in the front yard. A cluster of black flies hovered around a dead frog close to the hand pump. Rono stared at it and began to feel his legs. Melting again. The craving for whisky returned like a worm that had woken inside his head. He had to get it.

The shadows became closer and denser as Rono rode his bike along the unpaved quarter mile from his house to the bus stop. He looked at the road ahead. A bus had just trundled past. A few passengers had gotten off and now gathered around the bamboo mesh board displaying the day's newspaper. Rono headed to the corner store, the only one in the village. It sold everything from ribbons to rat poison. The store was deserted but for a couple of important-looking men in shades leaning against the glass counter, chatting with the cashier. Rono knew the cashier, a dark gaunt man in his twenties with a long narrow nose, the youngest of the owner's sons. The men in shades—strangers both, in their early twenties, beards trimmed sharp, dressed in dark jeans and homespun white tunics—stopped talking as he got closer, as though they were in the midst of a private conversation and had been intruded upon.

"Could I have that?" Rono said, cutting through the awkward silence.

"They're all empty. We're out of those," the cashier said,

not bothering to raise his head off the bamboo mesh tray where he was bundling up beedis in neat stacks.

"What are those then, sitting on your shelves?" Rono asked, pointing at the shiny, cellophane-wrapped cigarette cartons stacked neatly in the glass showcase behind the cashier.

"Those are for display," the cashier said.

One of the two men in shades looked away, feigning to suppress a giggle before the other broke into a loud laugh.

Rono went with the flow, laughing with them. "Give me a pack of those," he said again, pointing at the bundle of beedis the cashier was putting together.

"Those are sold," the cashier said.

"All of them?"

"There is a wedding uptown, they got them all."

"So you've nothing?"

"Nothing here." The cashier allowed a faint smile to flash past his flushed face as the two men laughed again.

There were no lights on the highway. The sky—pitch black. The two miles to the bazaar seemed like a long way. Rono had heard Rubina say to him once that a stretch on the highway was haunted. That was even before Dulal was hung up on the electric tower, not far from where Rono was right then. When he first heard that, he had simply laughed it off. Rubina had never been out this far after dark. She'd believe anything.

Rono's feet hit hard on the pedals. The station road was about eight feet wide, enough for a bus and a bullock cart to stand side by side. The asphalt on the road was loose, as though the people in charge of paving had run out of tar halfway into the job. It sat about six inches on top of the dirt, the edges on either side veering sharply off into the unpaved road bordering the bamboo thicket that ran the length of the highway to the bazaar. Rono held his bicycle closer to the centre of the road, straining to see through the dark. He'd have to rush to the side of the road the moment a vehicle came up from the front or back. With the moon eaten up by clouds, it was a struggle to see even a few feet ahead of him.

By the time Rono reached the bazaar, it was almost eight. The stores were preparing to close, all except the liquor store, where it was business as usual. Rono bought two quarts of whisky and two litre-sized bottles of Tiger, two packs of Navy Cut, and a book of matches. On his way back home, he felt a sense of relief, even triumph, manoeuvring his bike past the closed saree shops, six or seven of them huddled in a row. Past the underpass where a couple of schoolboys had confronted him, late in May, a week before the vote. He recalled the one with the long pointy face, shabby hair that looked almost like his own, wrapping his arm around his shoulder. "It'll be rough on the day of the vote. Stay home."

He could still feel the boy's hand resting on his shoulder. He could feel the hand sliding down his spine to the middle of his back, resting there a few seconds too long before pushing him away. "It's a war. We take care of war. You take care of home. You understand?"

Rono understood. He didn't care much about the vote anyway. Perhaps it was a mistake. He should have known better than to listen to Rubina. She said she had never been to a vote before. "I've never been anywhere." He knew she was right. They hadn't been anywhere at all since they got here.

"No one goes to a vote," one of his uncles had said.

"What if we do?" Rubina had yelled back at him.

"You vote. You pay."

That's it. He shouldn't have said that, Rono thought, feeling the breeze hit his face as he zipped back towards the highway. He liked the way his legs were moving now.

At the bus station, Haru was curled up inside his patched cape, claiming the entire cement bench near the newspaper stand. "Is that you?" he yelled as Rono passed him on his bike.

"Yes." Rono had noticed Haru, but as usual, he had not expected him to speak.

"Why did it take so long? Don't you have a wife at home to worry about?"

"Take how long?" Rono asked, bringing his bike to a stop, startled at being ambushed this late.

"I've been waiting," Haru said.

"Waiting for what?"

"For you to return."

"Return from where?"

"From the cake shop," he said, laughing out loud. "What did you get?" He rose abruptly to his feet, advancing rapidly towards Rono, who stood with the bike balanced between his legs.

"Cigarettes," Rono said.

"What else?"

"Tiger."

"And whisky?"

"A couple of quarts," Rono said, hurrying back onto his bike, irritated. "I got to go."

"Did you say Navy? Pass me one, will you?"

Rono looked at Haru—his large brown eyes shining in the haze of the solar lamp above the bus stand, wrinkles in the far corners of his eyes spread across his entire face as he stood there smiling. Quietly, Rono pulled a pack of cigarettes out of his breast pocket, felt the plastic overwrap, pulled the tear tape carefully, as if worried about the symmetry of the tear, flipped the lid of the pack, and popped a cigarette first in his own mouth, before he pulled another halfway out of the pack and held it out to Haru. Straightening the pedal of his bike with his foot, appearing to move away, he lighted up Haru's, then his own.

"Wait. I got something," Haru said, taking a deep drag from the cigarette before hurrying past the cement bench, sliding off into the brushwood behind the corner store for a few minutes, then reappearing back at the bus station with a cracked ceramic cup held out under Rono's nose. "Here, pour me some whisky."

"Whisky is for Sunday," Rono said.

"Come on, open the damn thing. I haven't had a decent drink all week."

Rono stared at Haru as he broke into a smile again. It seemed to Rono that Haru had been waiting all this time to say something, and he had no choice but to play along, find out. He sank his hand inside his sling bag and produced a plastic bottle of country spirit. Unscrewing the cap, he paused before taking a mouthful straight off the bottle and immediately regretted it, cringing as the raw spirit scorched his throat. Then, with barely open eyes, still recovering from the burn in his chest, he poured the Tiger, the colour of his grandfather's piss, into Haru's cup, screwed the cap back on, and waited. "Well?"

"I got something," Haru said, as he swung his cup to his mouth and held it there frozen for a few seconds, allowing the contents to drain completely. Then he dug into the pocket of his large cape and produced a piece of folded stationery. "I found this on your porch."

Unfolding it in small, deliberate gestures—almost knowing what to expect—Rono saw, in the light of the solar lamp, a hand-drawn swastika on a white sheet. "So. It's you," he said.

"They asked me to go get it, so I did. They said it'd be easy. But your wife wouldn't open the door."

"Get what?"

"Debts you owe. Didn't your wife tell you?"

"That man who can't stand up without a drink down his throat?" Rono said, his voice rising. "The man who has to let his wife on loan so he can have his morning hooch. He sent you to collect?"

"People at the Block sent me. He must have complained."

"What about the Block? Why are you giving this to me now?" Rono asked, his hand shaking as he held out the folded stationery before hurriedly putting it back in his pocket. "So this is what all this is about? A couple hundred bucks?"

Haru raised his cup, asking Rono to pour some more. Rono took another shot straight off the bottle, shutting his eyes to feel the burn snake down his throat, then splashed some more into Haru's cup. "Why do you think this is happening, Haru? First, they got Dulal, then they got Bishu Sen, and now they're after me. They did it once this morning. So why did they send you again?"

"Why ask me? Did you ask Bana why he refused to sell cigarettes with those two watching? You knew they were from the Block, didn't you? Did you ask them why?"

"Don't you ever ask them why?"

"I do what I'm told. I don't worry too much about the dead and the ghosts lined up on trees like bats or the blind like Bishu Sen—blind but still steaming on all engines after a mistress half his age."

"Bishu Sen will be back," Rono said with a firm shake of

his head, releasing his words one at a time like a hammer hitting a chisel, though he realized he had started to slur. "You can't keep a tiger pinned in a hole too long. You can tell them that."

"What would he come back for? He was ready to go the same day he saw Dulal up on the pole. Didn't you hear him on TV? Didn't you hear him cry out, 'Take me. Why don't you take me, you sons of bitches? Why did you leave me out?' He won't come back. He knew how the game is played. He made the rules. That bastard. He knows what's taken is taken."

"What do you mean taken? How can they just take him out like that?"

"That's what the rules are. They take what they want. When Bishu Sen was in the Block, he or his friends, for forty years, anything he wanted, he had. Anything he asked, he got it. Even a mistress. The ones in the Block now, what were they doing then? They hid in shitholes. Crawled like cockroaches. Now it's the cockroach's turn. They're out. They'll make him pay for not looking under the drains."

"Where have they taken him?"

"Not just him—his house, his goats and cows and fish, and the cabinet loaded with imported liquor—whatever he left behind. And the chairs and tables and lamps, the beds and mattresses, sheets and pillows, pots and pans, plates, pictures, all taken. They'll all go."

"What would they do with stuff out of a burnt house?"

"Burnt, my ass. Did you ever go inside? Go ask the boys when they get there tonight. Every night. Drinking his whisky, playing his cards, spinning his records, courting visitors, getting laid in his bed. Yes, that too. Everything's taken. Everything will have to go. They have it all worked out."

"Why are you telling me this?"

"I'm not telling you anything you haven't asked."

"The boys meet up at Bishu Sen's house every night, and no one knows a thing. That burnt house? Everyone saw the smoke. Did you or did you not? Some thugs make a grab at a hundred years' history—his things, his friends, all those folks he shared his drinks with—every evening. You mean they don't know? They've sewn their mouths, all of them. You idiot, what do you think they're waiting for? For the same to happen to them. You live here in this shithole like a shit fly, and you think that's how things work. That's not how things work. Bishu Sen will return and then all the thugs stealing off him, they'd have to slime back into the drain."

"What about you? Aren't you his friend?"

"I was no friend, just family. Not close anyway, just a splice in the bloodline."

"See. They know that. Everyone knows that. Bishu Sen has no friends, an oversexed blind man. He's over. But you? You're here. You're not stupid. That's why you're alive. You can't be stupid and expect to be alive. No one can afford that," Haru said, raising his cup for a refill and letting the wrinkles in his face explode once more as he smiled. "Here, why don't you open the whisky. It's been weeks since I've had anything decent. They took everything away, those bastards, everything out of the blind man's cabinet, even the quart I hid in the commode."

Rono ignored Haru and poured some more Tiger into his raised cup. Haru sipped slowly, slurping as though it were piping hot. "Who can you trust? Look at this damn Tiger. This piss, what good is it? I can't stand up straight. Other than that, what did it do? It hasn't done a damn thing yet," Haru said. "Not yet. Pour some more." He raised the cup out again, leaning onto Rono, grabbing his shoulder to stand himself straight.

Rono filled it halfway.

"Fill it up," Haru demanded.

Rono poured more into Haru's raised cup, as if in a spell, before screwing the cap back onto the nearly empty bottle of Tiger, whisking it into his sling bag again. He didn't want to stay any longer. He could hear the crickets buzz in his ears. His breathing had become louder. He could hear that. He could sense his hand shaking on the bike's handlebar. He could feel his muscles cramping.

"What's gone is gone, why do you care? History gone back to history, what good is that? History gone back to people; there's good in that. It'd make the old man happy. No one's after you. What do you have? A taste for booze? You've a taste for vote? Debts. You've got a pretty wife. Don't they know that? They know what you have. If they want it, they'll take it. If you want to get all shaken up, they'd send someone to calm you down. Stop worrying. You're safe. No one will touch you. No one will dare touch you," Haru said, dragging himself away.

"Why won't they touch me?" Rono asked.

"Because you're not stupid. Ask your wife. She took care of it. She's the right kind of smart. You're a lucky man. She took care of it all, and you don't know. You've nothing to worry about, and you don't know. Go home. Go back home. Show her that piece of paper. She'll know what that is. She knows what must be done to turn the mark around. To have it face the right way. She knows when it's faced right, it's all good. That's when all debts are paid. She knows that. She might have been told. She might tell you. Or she might not. But I'm telling you. Just leave the bottle behind. I'll have it washed."

As Rono stared down the narrow, unpaved exit to B-Col, a civet walked the length of the dark patch near the corner store, sliding off the edge into the brushwood. It was past ten. Rono didn't want to go home yet. He decided to head down to Bishu Sen's, not past his own home but through the hidden entrance at the back, facing the highway.

Barely able to carry his weight on the bike, he kept cutting in and out, trailing off the sharp edges of the highway onto the dirt before getting back on, his vision blurry, his head numb with the constant thrum of crickets. He did that a few times before a truck avoiding a dog veered off the middle of the road and zipped past, almost knocking him over. A sudden rush of adrenalin hit him in the head, waking him instantly.

Inside Bishu Sen's estate, he could see for the first time the burnt facade of the house. A set of low steps wound around the outer columns of the house like a ring. As he walked in, he saw a thick layer of damp soot covering the hallway on the ground level. A nest of mice scurried through the flashlight beam as he pointed his phone at the corners. The stairway that started halfway up the hallway was pocked with circular pits of dirt around a busy network of footprints. He trained his flashlight up the stairway. Footprints ran up to the landing of the second floor. He had climbed those stairs countless times. He followed the prints to the second level that opened into the lobby. The door facing the lobby stood shut tight. He stood there awhile, of two minds, listening in. There were no signs of damage in the upper level. Everything seemed intact—mirrors, paintings, plaques, plates, photo frames—just the way he had seen them when he was last here, only six weeks earlier.

As he pushed the doors open, he thought he saw Bishu Sen reclined on the divan, his head supported by a pillow under the crook of his arm; Bishu Sen's glazed eyes staring blankly at the TV. The TV was still plugged in; a film of dust on the opaque screen lit up as Rono drew an arc with his flashlight around the walls of the lobby. He knew the doors on either side led to a series of interconnected rooms that ran like a chain along the girth of the house. He had never been inside the rooms before. He knew the north door from the lobby led to the crescent balcony out front.

Facing the divan, a suite of wooden chairs around the glass table lay exactly as he had seen them last as if Bishu Sen had invited his friends, the same old faces, and they had scurried back into the shadows upon seeing Rono, the forever outsider. A thick sooty film sat on everything in the arc of the flashlight-lit lobby—cabinets inside the walls, books on open shelves, busts and figurines, corners of tables—everything coated in dust and soot except the seats of the chairs; the floor underneath, pocked with footprints. It seemed to him Bishu Sen was staring at him, waiting for him to leave so he could resume court with his band of coots, or perhaps ask Rono to hang on, finish what he started—the bust that would become green in the courtyard outside.

As he walked into the adjoining room, he saw a folded mosquito net hung on the bedpost like a canopy, a crumpled sheet hanging from the corner of the bed. As he pushed the window, it opened with a loud crack onto the balcony. He could see his own house a few hundred yards away. The night lay before his eyes, dark and opaque and plugged in, like the TV. A dull glare from a half-hidden moon had settled on the roofs and cornices of B-Col, as though it were liquid, needing a place to rest and resist the pull into the ground where it'd be wasted. He must return home, Rono thought. He didn't want to be found up here, alone on the balcony.

Back home, he slid off his bike. Careful not to make even the slightest sound, he sat on the front stairs under the porch. It was quiet inside the house. He didn't want to go in yet, didn't have to, wasn't ready. Bi must have gone to sleep waiting for him, he thought. Looking into the dark courtyard, he opened a quart of whisky. He'd stay outside, waiting for them. He'd catch them in the act and that would be that.

Then, for a moment, he thought of returning to Number 14 and setting it on fire—this time for real. He looked for his book of matches. They were right there. But his feet felt heavy. His mind dead still. He lighted up a match stick. A soft easterly breeze swept through the leaves. Blew it out. He looked into the sky. Maybe it was going to rain again, heavy and swift like the moonlit showers he saw outside the tall, pristine glass windows of Stoney Creek as Gina Farina held her camera out, their heads almost touching, as she hit her long, painted nail on the lighted screen of the camera to move the starry night sky along, so much more quickly than he liked. He fumbled as he struck the match again and as the matchstick lit up, he watched the flare and imagined it's the big house burning.

2020

LORNE PARK

—KAL

Sisters

Aunt Rita is my first mother. Lately, I've been the only one visiting her at the Sunset Village three times a week. But when she passed, Mam decided Aunt Rita's first son, Auro Tomorrow, would press the red button at the Brampton Crematorium. He was called Auro Tomorrow for a reason. If Mam needed him today, he'd show up in a week. And even now, when the family is planning Aunt Rita's funeral, he isn't here. No one knows yet if he will show up for the cremation at all. Mam is Aunt Rita's younger sister, but on matters concerning Aunt Rita, Mam's decision is final.

Thirty-five years ago, Mam had sponsored Aunt Rita to Canada. Since then, Mam gives the impression that she owns her, even though they haven't talked for years, even though Aunt Rita is dead and they can't talk anymore, even though Aunt Rita has two children of her own living across town—Auro Tomorrow and Toshie Noshie. Toshie rarely talks. She's so poor, everyone avoids her. And there is no one else to question Mam's verdict about who presses the red button. No one except Smelly Snelly, Mam's own daughter and my half-sister. Snelly was first to let me in on this complicated family situation—"My dad and your dad is the same person." She's the only one who wants me to press the red button.

"Bitter?" Snelly asks when she finds me alone at the foyer of Sunset Village, Aunt Rita's nursing home. Snelly is a food scientist. At work, she maps emotions to taste. Outside, she treats it like a game. I am an accountant, I don't have to play her game.

"Can you name it?"

"No."

"Name it." Snelly has a short fuse, too. She's annoying.

"Pretzels," I say, just to get her off me. But I don't feel anything. And I haven't cried. There is nothing to cry for. No memories except that I've been visiting her for three years since the day Snelly made it very clear for me—"My dad, who is your Uncle Fatik, made Aunt Rita pregnant, and then you happened." I never had to explain to Aunt Rita why I was showing up three times a week all of a sudden. I doubt she knew who I was. Her language had declined. We have never talked.

"I'm grapefruit." Snelly crinkles her nose to show disgust. She says she can tell I'm hurting, but I know she cannot. Because I'm not hurting at all. But Snelly thinks she owns me. She tells me everything. Like one day three years ago, when the nursing home panicked over a choking incident, she told me about Aunt Rita and Uncle Fatik and then tried to convince Mam to visit her sister. We were sitting in the kitchen. In the half-hour, Snelly had finished a whole bag of Extra Spicy Doritos dipped in pasta sauce. More like a tub of pasta sauce dipped in Extra Spicy Doritos. When the nursing home called again, she tried to vomit it all out like a wine taster. She didn't tell anyone else what she was feeling. Snelly says spicy is anger, anxiety, fear.

"Shouldn't it work the other way?"

"Which other way?"

"Shouldn't you be eating ice cream when you're angry?"

Snelly likes to feel it when she's feeling it. Another time it was a bag of freshly sliced lunch meat while she waited in her car outside a *psychic* store. Mam was inside, looking at a crystal ball in order to find out the exact sequence of events during that one week when she'd had to travel to Ottawa for training and leave the husband behind with the sister.

Aunt Rita was fifty-four when I was born. That was five years after Uncle Fatik started the second Fat's Convenience in Meadowvale, and Mam became a full-time pharmacy assistant at Costco, and Aunt Rita fell down in a bathroom somewhere in India, lost an eye, left her husband, and moved into the attic of her sister's Lorne Park house. Snelly was a latchkey girl then, the family needed Aunt Rita. Back then, Aunt Rita's own daughter lived fifteen minutes west. But Aunt Rita preferred to live at her sister's. Snelly says it was because of "her affair with dad."

Exactly one year later, Aunt Rita would be asked to pack her things and clear out. Mam says it was Aunt Rita's choice to leave me behind as she moved into a basement with her daughter, whose family had fallen into hard times due to the husband's gambling and drinking and stuff that no one ever talks about. Snelly says Aunt Rita was given no choice; everyone hated her. Snelly says there is no specific taste for hate because hate is a hybrid emotion, made of fear and anger.

Before Snelly moved to London, Ontario, her house in Brampton was the place I'd hide whenever the thought occurred to me that I was really the other child. In her study, she had a chart showing all kinds of emotions mapped to all kinds of food: warheads ➡ envy; sardines ➡ sadness; jalapeño ➡ surprise. "You're the reason I couldn't have a child," she once said to me. She's a liar. I don't believe that.

She's fourteen years older. That's one year more than the gap between Mam and Aunt Rita, who turned eighty-six before she passed. That makes Mam seventy-three. But when I say, "Mam has started forgetting things," Snelly says, "Don't ever say it again." She wants everyone to last forever. So she must be hurting. Because Aunt Rita is gone.

In our particular tradition, when someone dies, you grieve for thirteen days. But since Auro Tomorrow has just arrived and also has to get back to his new wife waiting for him in their renovated one-dollar house in Italy, Mam decided the grieving would last seven days. After that, the wake. It makes no sense to adjust grief to a calendar, but about Aunt Rita, Mam's word is final.

"Call everyone," she orders, pausing the blender where

she is beating eggs and cream of tartar for sugar-free meringue cookies. Mam is diabetic. Sweet can kill her. But she likes to bake. A month ago, she was making macarons when Snelly said Aunt Rita might respond to old pictures. Mam called the nursing home to ask why they were spreading lies. Unlike Snelly, Mam doesn't like to feel anything, unless she has to.

Aunt Rita had been in a wheelchair in Sunset since 2007. Thirteen years. Her nurse says she remembers things in flashes—mostly food, from many years past—because she talks about it right after—not the time and place she ate something, but that something was not sweet. Sweet is the only taste she remembers. Snelly says pride stopped Aunt Rita from returning to get me. Pride tastes sweet.

Last week when everyone knew Aunt Rita would be gone soon, Snelly offered to bring to the nursing home some possessions she had left behind. Mam asked me if I brought the cheesecake she likes. She likes to talk sweet when she doesn't want to talk.

"What good would it do, do you think?" Mam was lounging in the yard, absent-mindedly finishing a pencil portrait of a dead relative. Mam and other members of the clan have decided to curate dead family members; tether them all inside a book with portraits and bios.

"What about me? " I asked in jest.

"Are you dead?" Snelly played along. "Your portrait will need colour, though." She is always complaining I'm too pale.

"Talking may slow down the forgetting," Mam said without raising her head from the portrait.

"She doesn't remember much," I said, hoping Mam would visit and Aunt Rita would ask about me.

"When you're sick like her, you don't remember. You only forget. But that's something she earned." Mam has her own way of finishing a conversation.

Mam's ears become red when she's out in the sun long. It's July and the smoke from the fires in Northern Ontario has put the air in a chokehold. Now inside, she holds the casserole containing the sugar-free cheesecake I got her. She has been asking for it habitually ever since I ran into the owner of the old bakery, three blocks from home.

When I showed photos, the bakery owner said he knew Mam.

"What about Aunt Rita?"

"They never came together, but they always asked for the same thing." It's remarkable he even remembered. Perhaps he made it up. Perhaps there weren't many that looked like them. He said he'd do the cheesecake sugar-free.

Mam cut the cake into perfect squares and covered them individually in cling wrap. She is saving them for the funeral. She is going to have the crematorium tray them by the coffee.

Not many came to the funeral. Actually, no one other than those who couldn't stay away—Mam and me and Auro

Tomorrow and Toshie Noshie. And there was Philomena, her nurse for the past three years. She sat by herself in a black lace dress, her lips painted cherry as if she was expecting a crowd and needed to stand out among strangers with stronger claims on the patient she cared for. Her hair had a bright, new shine as if she'd had it coloured just before she got there, carefully styled. She must have gone to a hairdresser for it. She cried like she had lost someone she knew well. Or because of what she knew. Or because it was the end of what she knew. I had met her several times at the nursing home. It could be all three. I don't know. Sometimes you cry because others are crying. Maybe Snelly knew that. She didn't come.

At the crematorium, Mam wore dark glasses. It must have been the fluorescents with that electric hum, mixed with the sound of hymns piping out of hidden speakers. The lino floor was so shiny, our shoes squeaked; the flowers in the reception, freshly cut; the girl at the front entrance in a black suit, businesslike, eager to please—"what would you like? what would you like?" Everything was neatly arranged, even the haze from the sandalwood incense hovering over the hallway, shaped like a humongous meringue. Snelly says, "Dying is just like dessert. You die to remember the meal."

The crematorium had questions. Since we hadn't ordered in advance—will a standard white wreath do? What about the casket—would we like to rent or buy? What would be the duration of visitations? Is the air conditioning all right? Will there be older guests? Should they move the cheesecakes into the prayer room? Do we have any preference for prayer tracks?

Then they explained the sequence of events, even though Mam seemed to know. Mam, being the official clan elder, is supposed to know everything. The visitation was to be followed by prayers. Yes, the crematorium could arrange a priest. A firepit would be okay, so long as we took care of the smoke. Yes, the casket could be opened after the prayers one last time. Then it'd be taken to the area at the back where the ovens work night and day. "Perhaps you can hear them now." Perhaps the incessant humming was the ovens and not the fluorescent lights. Only ten close family members were allowed. The urn was to be retrieved in a week after the ash cools down. Do we have a photo? We did. It was quaint. From a time before she got here. Aunt Rita and her other children playing in the rain. Her black hair tied firmly in a knot behind her neck. Water standing still like pieces of broken glass on the part of her hair.

It was a Wednesday. There were others dead. Other halls had more people.

"Where's Snelly?" Mam asked.

"Snelly isn't coming," I said. She had said she'd come, then she changed her mind.

"Why," I had asked. She didn't answer. But now I know. Had she seen Philomena crying, she'd have felt it, and she'd have to eat Extra Spicy Doritos dunked in a tub of pasta sauce.

Snelly didn't speak English when she got here. She used to have a lisp. Now she talks weirdly. And really fast, as if by talking fast she can spit out whatever it is she wishes to say without being interrupted. Strange for a person who likes to feel it when she's feeling it. Snelly says there is no official taste for grief. It could be a lie. Because after I saw Philomena at the crematorium, my mouth tasted like metal. Everything is a lie, anyway.

I was born here, nine years after Snelly arrived from India. She's my half-sister, but we're neither the same colour nor taste. She's coffee; I'm wheat. She's olives and tabasco—half and half; I'm rhubarb and kimchi. Envy, anxiety, shame—she has it all mapped out on her board. She said she'd be there for the wake.

One day, we were having sundaes when Snelly said she got old too soon because Mam had her when she was twenty-seven. Now she wants to sell everything and retire with Mam.

"Why so early?"

"You have a problem with that?"

I do. Because Snelly wants to sell the house we live in. Mam has willed it to her. But I've lived here all my life. We don't talk about it.

"You can live with us in Florida," she says.

I'm thirty-two. It's not the same.

The house is a 1959 craftsman bungalow. Mam and Uncle Fatik bought it in 1981 when Lorne Park was still a little village. Nothing here goes for less than two million now. Mam is proud.

"Why can't she be proud about a house in Lorne Park? This was what she came here for. Get rich. Get richer," Snelly says. But the truth is, that's what she's left with—a house in Lorne Park.

Mam would take anyone on a tour, even the chimney sweep. There is a method. She'd start from the stairway near the main entrance, work her way up to the landing on the upper floor. She'd talk about the reinforced ceiling, the jatoba wood of the floor, the polished metal railings. She'd stop often, point at the walls around the stairwell and the landing crowded with photos of Uncle Fat and her and Snelly. My photos, too, but only after I had grown a moustache—no photos on a tricycle or in a splash pad—as if she was waiting for something to happen before she could let me in. Not until after Aunt Rita was sent to Sunset. Aunt Rita makes pretty photos. Her photos are banned. At the end of the tour, Mam would offer a piece of homemade saltwater taffy from an airtight container.

Friday morning, a day before the wake, Snelly pulls up in the driveway. She must have started out early. Mam and I are still at breakfast. Snelly says she forgot something and goes out to retrieve a box of blood oranges. She zests them with a potato peeler, runs a cleaver carefully through the pith, between segments, puts them on boil. She doesn't remove the seeds. The juice turns out the colour of blood.

Bitter as bitter. She adds loads of sugar to compensate, but that never works. Mam won't touch it. She puts it in a crystal jar and places it on the dining table as if she just wants to look at it. Mam hates bitter. Mam thinks Snelly is slowly bittering away. She never told me that. Mam doesn't tell me anything. But I know from the way she looks at Snelly before walking away towards the fridge, poking her head into the freezer. Mam is lost.

Why would Smelly Snelly do something like that?

"I don't know," she says. "I like the colour."

"It looks like blood." I knew it wasn't about the colour.

"It sure would taste like blood when its ready." Snelly looks out the window.

"Soon there will be flies."

"Flies can't see red, you nutcase."

"But they sure can taste the sugar. Can't they?"

"That's why I left the seed. Do you want to try?"

"Flies do come for the bitter sometimes."

"Only when things get complicated."

"And what do you do then?"

"Leave it alone. That's the only way to deal with it." Snelly poured yeast into the blood orange and left it to ferment. The dark circles under her eyes lit up when she faced the window.

The night Mam called Toshie Noshie, Aunt Rita's daughter, and asked her to take her mother away, I was one, probably sucking a teether in my sleep. Smelly Snelly, my half-sister, my keeper, was fifteen. She says she was with me. When Aunt Rita realized she was being banished for good, Snelly says, Aunt Rita locked herself in the washroom. Then she had to be rushed to the hospital because she had gashed her face. As if her movie-star looks, even with the blue false eye, were the only reason for all the trouble. The scar was still there when they opened the casket at the crematorium for the last time. Some things just don't heal.

"What's wrong with you?" Mam gets annoyed when she sees flies.

"What about Aunt Rita?" Snelly holds one end of a charcoal portrait Mam has been working on.

"What *about* her?"

"Your own sister dies in a hospital less than two miles from here, all you've been doing is portraits of dead people, and something is wrong with *me*?"

"We're doing just men." Mam looks away.

"What's wrong with crying?" Snelly looks at me as though it's all my fault.

"Why wouldn't she take me?" I ask Snelly.

"Go ask Mam why she kept you here."

"Mam says I belong here."

"Let me hear it. I want to hear it from her."

"What's inside your mouth, sour herring or rotten egg?"

"You should be crying, you rockhead." Snelly gets upset

when people don't feel things like she wants them to feel.

"You can't pretend as if I'm the only one not feeling anything." I don't get her.

"Mam has her reasons."

"Mam has her house."

"Is that what you think this is about? A frigging house?"

"I'm not going anywhere."

"You're coming with us. Say thank you."

Mam wears the same black dress for the wake that she wore at the funeral.

Snelly orders nasturtiums. "Look what I got."

"What do I need flowers for?" Mam sits by the window watching a squirrel eat her tomatoes.

"You can eat them, you know?"

"Who eats flowers?"

"Slugs do."

"Are they blind?"

"They're not legally blind, but they've got their eyes on top of their head."

"What do they taste like?"

"Watercress."

"What is the taste of watercress?"

"Bell pepper."

"Rita likes bell pepper. I mean, she used to like it." Mam fusses about carrying the cheque book.

"Why are *you* paying for Aunt Rita's wake when Auro is here?"

"She's my charge. I got her here."

"Stop the farce. Everyone is laughing at us," Snelly says.

"Who is everyone?" I ask.

Then Snelly shows me the phone book packed with uncles, aunts, cousins I know nothing about.

During the wake, when Auro Tomorrow is asked to make a speech, he says he owes it to his blood that he needs more sweet than others to get to the same level of happiness. Toshie Noshie says she is too full of emotion to say anything coherent. Snelly says, to balance all the sweetness in the bloodline she made blood orange wine. Someone laughs. Everyone knows Snelly has a loose screw. Then Snelly looks at me. "Now my brother Kal will say something important," she says. I don't have anything to say. I wasn't expecting to have to say anything. "She was lucid when I last met her. She knew why I was there. She raised a hand, she was trying to say something—go away; listen to me; I forgive you." People nod, as if they can tell it's a lie. Mam looks away. Philomena says Aunt Rita was always the first one to show up in the big dining hall so long as her hands could steer the wheels of her own chair. She says Aunt Rita always managed to corner the tub of marmalade. She says Aunt Rita loved cheesecakes, most of all. She'd cut a slice into the smallest possible bits, take one piece, save the rest, and forget about it until it'd all turn bad with fungus, and then she would cry.

Mam wears dark glasses again. Mam doesn't say a

word. "Where's Snelly?" she asks. "Who's handing out the cheesecakes today?"

"There are no cheesecakes today," I say. I saw Snelly leaving the hall right after Philomena was done speaking. I can tell something is wrong. I know Snelly had walked out of the house the day Aunt Rita was let go. Then they found Snelly collapsed on the ice. Snelly was Aunt Rita's only friend in Lorne Park. I know Snelly is feeling it. It's hard not to feel it after listening to Philomena. I go looking for Snelly.

There she is by the cooler. Pouring out her bitter blood orange in tiny goblets. I guess she wants to make sure everyone gets a taste of how *she*'s feeling. There is no point. Snelly's such a showboat. I am not going to take it. I am not going to argue with her either.

ACKNOWLEDGEMENTS

Many thanks to the editors of the journals where some of the stories first appeared, sometimes in different forms.

"The Man and the Boy" in *Black Fox Literary Journal*

"Let's Not Talk About AB" in *Rice Paper*

"Pumpkin Flowers" in *Anomaly*

"Sisters" in *Punt Volat*

Thanks to my teachers Stella Harvey, David Bergen, and the faculty in the creative writing program at the University of British Columbia for their time and energy. I'm grateful to Wendy Atkinson for her generous support and encouragement. Thanks to Pearl Luke for her perception and insight and to Heather Tekavec for her patience and keen eye, and David Lester and Julie Cochrane for the design, and Kevin Welsh for his attentiveness and wisdom. Immense gratitude to Ontario Arts Council and Diaspora Dialogues for their generous grant that made it possible for me to write this book. Above all, thanks to my family and friends for their support, indulgence, kindness, and encouragement.

ABOUT THE AUTHOR

Sabyasachi (Sachi) Nag is the author of three collections of poetry including *Uncharted* (Mansfield Press, 2021) and *Could You Please, Please Stop Singing* (Mosaic Press, 2015). His work has appeared in *Anomaly*, *Black Fox Literary*, *Canadian Literature*, *Grain*, *The Antigonish Review*, *The Dalhousie Review* and *The Windsor Review* among other places. An alumnus of the Banff Centre's Literary Arts program, Sachi holds creative writing certificates from the Writer's Studio at Simon Fraser University and from Humber College. He is currently an MFA candidate at the University of British Columbia. He is grateful to have the opportunity to live with his wife and son in Mississauga, which is part of the Treaty Lands and Territory of the Mississaugas of the Credit, the Anishinaabeg, the Chippewa, the Haudenosaunee, and the Wendat peoples and is now home to many diverse First Nations, Inuit, and Métis peoples. You can find him at sachiwrites.com.